BROKEN
sparrow

A chance encounter. An unlikely hero.

www.chellebliss.com

CHELLE BLISS
USA TODAY BESTSELLING AUTHOR

BROKEN SPARROW © 2021

Publisher © Bliss Ink October 5th 2021
Edited by Lisa A. Hollett
Proofread by Read By Rose
Cover Design © Chelle Bliss
Cover Photo © FuriousFotog
Cover Model Wesley Dutchman

To all the women who want more...

OPEN ROAD SERIES

Book 1 - Broken Sparrow (Morris)
Book 2 - Broken Dove (Leo)
Book 3 - Broken Wings (Crow)
Book 4 - Broken Arrow (Arrow)

The Open Road series is interconnected with the
Men of Inked: Heatwave series. Learn more at
menofinked.com/heatwave-series

Also available in alternative paperback

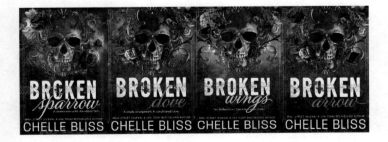

CHAPTER
ONE
MORRIS

"YOU SURE ABOUT THIS GUY? 'Cuz all you have to do is say the word…"

I'm sitting on my bike, parked in front of the entrance to the gas station. The late morning sun hits my face. There is silence on the end of the line, and that makes me sweat worse than the Florida sun.

I don't like it when she goes silent.

It means she's afraid.

"Jessica…baby," I urge. "I know you said this one is different, but if he's turning out to be anything like that motherfucker ex of yours—"

"Morris, no. God, no. Nothing like that."

I can't make out the hesitant tone in Jessica's voice. What it means. What she's feeling. There was something there with Jessica. Her sweetness, the way she looked at me like I was the answer to all her prayers. Maybe not old lady material… She had shit of her own to sort out, but she opened up something in me that kept me checking in on her.

Fuck it, I cared about her. And the phone sex was out-of-this-world hot. Her sweet voice whispering my name, the tremble I could hear when she made herself come for me, so wicked over the phone. My dick tightened in my jeans just thinking about it. But eventually, the calls started dropping off. Our plans to meet up in person never came together.

Then two months ago, she dropped the bomb. She'd met someone. Really met someone.

"Baby," I growl into the phone. "Level with me. He treating you good? At least as good as I would? Because I swear to fuck…"

Jessica barks a soft laugh over the line. "There's no one like you, Morris," she says softly, wistfully. "That's the problem." Her voice grows a little stronger as she says his name. "Kyle is a good one," she assures me. "He's not you, Morris. But it's good. *He's* good. JD even likes him, which is sayin' something."

I listen for clues in her voice, unsure if what I'm hearing is honesty or uncertainty. "Yeah?" I press. "If JD doesn't have an issue with him…" I echo, not ready to believe she bounced from her shitty ex Boyd to Prince Kyle Fucking Charming in one go.

Her son JD, Mammoth to me, would sniff out an asshole and chase his ass far away. If he hasn't done it yet, then I have to believe Kyle is a solid guy. Since Mammoth and Jessica reconnected after years of living apart, Mammoth hasn't taken his eyes off her… one of the reasons we didn't spend more time together.

He didn't think I was the right fit for his mom and he was right. I wasn't the type she needed or deserved.

I must sound like I don't believe her, because she talks over me. "You're one of the best ones, Morris. And Kyle is too," she reminds me. "If I sound funny, it's because—"

"Jessica." I cut her off. I can't explain the static in my brain when I think about Jessica being trapped again in some bullshit relationship with a good-for-nothing douchebag.

She's better than that. She has to know that by now.

A woman in black yoga pants with sunglasses on her face rushes past me and into the gas station. Her steps set off the sliding doors, which open and blast me with a gust of air-conditioned relief.

"Morris, if I sound a little off…" Jessica continues.

I kick a leg over my bike and pat my pocket for my wallet. This may not be a conversation I should continue inside, but my neck is starting to sweat and I need to take a leak.

"Yeah," I say, "you do, sugar."

I walk through the doors of the gas station, the whoosh of the doors drowning out Jessica's soft apology. I scan the aisles, looking for the head. I've never been to this place before, a midsized gas station off the interstate between Daytona and Orlando, and I'm just hoping I don't need to ask the teenager wearing green glitter eye shadow up to his eyebrows for a key so I can piss.

"Go on, sweetheart," I say low into the phone, spotting the restroom sign and heading toward the far back corner of the gas station. "Level with me. Just say what you gotta say."

"I'm so sorry, Morris," she says. "It's just that… It's serious. Kyle and I moved in together. I can't have…male friends or at least I shouldn't."

Can't have male friends.

I roll my eyes. This Kyle guy's douchebag status shoots into the stratosphere. Whether he is a controlling dick or an insecure one doesn't matter to me.

"I ain't nobody's male friend," I say, the words sour in my mouth. I yank the doorknob to the single bathroom, and it sticks. "Did that fucker say you can't have male friends? Because if he did, that's some bullshit."

"Occupied!" a voice calls out from inside when the handle doesn't budge.

I lean against the wall to wait.

"No, not exactly, but I think it's best for my heart and the sake of my future if we cut our communication down to a minimum. Kyle isn't exactly thrilled—"

"Jess," I say, "I get it. New guy doesn't want old

dick circling his bitch," I explain. "Look, I want you happy. You deserve to be happy." I hear the sound of the air dryer, and I know relief is in sight. "And I get that old...*friends*...can cause trouble where there is none, all right?" I scrub a hand over my forehead, wipe the sweat from the bridge of my nose, and tug the sunglasses from my face. I tuck them in the front pocket of my leather vest and sigh. "Listen. You find yourself in a bad way, you call me. Night or day. We clear? One wrong move from that asshole, and I'll be down there so fast..."

I can hear her suck a deep breath on the other end of the line. "Morris..." she says, sadness coating her tone. "I don't want this to be goodbye."

"Baby, I'm happy for you. Make that asshole treat you right. You deserve nothing less than the best." I nod, not that she can see me, but because this is right for her. I'm not a keeping man. She wanted things I could never give her. Maybe this Kyle would. "But, sweetheart," I purr low into the phone.

"Oh... Excuse me." Yoga pants girl yanks open the bathroom door, her eyes widening as she sees me waiting against the wall.

I nod at her and step aside to make a little more room. She drops her eyes to the black-and-white checkerboard tile as she scurries past.

"Don't delete my number, Jess," I say. "You hear?" Something twists in my chest, a small shudder as I realize this really is goodbye.

"I won't, Morris," she promises. "You be good."

I bark a laugh and yank on the door to the now-available head. "Never," I vow.

I end the call and relieve myself, blinking away the emotions the conversation brought out.

Fuck… Can't say I'm sad. Can't say I'm *feeling* much of anything.

Jessica was one of those women like so many over the years. No. I can't lie to myself about that. She wasn't like the others. There was something about her.

A connection that maybe, just maybe, could have lasted past a couple of nights filled with whiskey and no-strings sex.

But like she told me, she still wants stability and safety. A life that is more than the ride and the chase.

Panty-melting fucking and liquor don't exactly measure up to all the trappings of a life I couldn't give her. Wouldn't give her. All the things she wants she'd never have with me.

I rinse my hands and shake them dry, letting the restroom door slam shut behind me. I'm happy for Jess.

Nah, not that. Not happy.

But she laid down the law, and I'll abide by it. She had something going with this guy and a… Fuck, a *male friend* putting his dick where it didn't belong… For now, Jessica says she's good, and that's good enough for me. It has to be.

I head toward the coolers for a bottle of something for the road. I've got another half-hour ride ahead to the property, and that sun is going to hit hard by the time I reach the isolated yard. Better fuel up with more than just gas while I'm here.

The club is changing. Has to. With Crow locked up, we're down a man, and we need what every club needs—manpower and cash.

And more than that, I'm not looking to spend the rest of my life locked up behind bars. The Disciples aren't the same, sliding further into illegal activities, upping my chances of dying inside a jail cell.

Six months ago, we decided to break away from the Disciples and start a new club. It wasn't an easy vote, but it's what is best for us and our future.

We are no longer the Disciples or any dangling branch of the original club.

We are new.

Born fresh.

Starting over from scratch.

We are going legit, making money the old-fashioned way without the complications of drugs and violence. Looking over our shoulders had become tiring, but I'm sure the habit will take years to shake.

I've spent the last couple months fucking Jessica by phone at night and securing a real estate deal by day. Using part of the club's cash reserves, we bought a small commercial property at a real estate auction. Practically stole that shit.

The bank seized a C-3 zoned strip with loads of parking on nearly two acres of land. The listing only said the existing building has PVC air lines inside, which made me think auto repair or auto service. All I saw of the building itself before we made the offer was one grainy aerial photo on the auction listing. We bought the whole nine with cash, as-is. Everything, including any trash, leftover equipment, lock, stock, and barrel, all ours as of closing.

When the club decided to expand, we couldn't agree on exactly what we'd put on the new property, but we don't really know what'll work until we can gain access to the place and figure out if anything left is usable. Or if we have to demo the whole site and start from scratch. I can't say I care either way.

Tattoo shops and cars, the shit we know best, they don't need foot traffic to bring in business. But I've been wondering about whether we should try something a little different. Diversify a bit. Still cash-heavy shit like auto repair or, fuck, maybe even a nail salon, something the old ladies of the club can benefit from too. Anything that can move a little money when we need to, but something that will also bring in dollars clean.

Legit.

As I head toward the coolers, I spot the girl from the bathroom. She's standing in front of the hot dog machine, shuffling back and forth on her feet, looking like she's got the weight of the world riding on this decision. She's got her hand deep in what looks like a child's purse, and she's digging through it, like she's scrounging for change.

Maybe it's the curve of her ass in those body-hugging pants or the fact that her hair is almost the same shade as the sunshine, but I walk up to her.

"Pick the one with the pucker," I say.

She turns her full body toward me, looking startled. "Excuse me?" She closes the small purse and grasps it to her chest like I'm a mugger sizing up her tiny teal handbag for what's inside.

I give her a playful grin. I point past her to the slim rolls of meat, each one slowly turning under an electric heat lamp.

"Pick the one with the pucker," I repeat. "See the skin?" I nod toward the glass display case where the hot dogs are in various states of doneness. "That one." I lean down to point to the one I mean, and I catch a whiff of her hair. She smells sweet, like cookies. Pure sugar. "When the skin puckers like that, it means the dog is nice and cooked inside but not too dry and not too raw. Just right," I explain.

The woman watches me and takes a tiny step back. I get it. I'm a heavily tattooed stranger three times her size, and she's a sweet little wisp of a thing trying to buy her lunch in peace. She's pushed her sunglasses up onto her head, and I can see her brown eyes are light, startlingly so. The look of caution in them, and the tightness at her mouth, trip up my gut.

I can see the light dim in her face as she scans my beard, my leathers, the decades-old ink on my neck.

She's braced. Protective. Afraid.

And that's my cue to move on.

"Cover it up with some relish and you got damn near as decent a meal as you can get on the road." I give her a grin and a nod, ending the conversation.

She gives me a press of her lips that passes for smiling back, but it's guarded. Hesitant. She looks like she's struggling between being polite and running for her life. It hits me why I'm drawn to her, why I'm chatting up a sexy stranger in front of the hot dog machine at a gas station.

Jessica. This woman reminds me of Jessica. No old lady, not one of those down-to-whatever, whenever, for-a-good-time types.

She's another scared little bird fallen from the nest. If only women like this understood what real wolves look like.

I take one last breath of that sugar-cookie fragrance. "Enjoy your dog," I say.

Then she speaks. "Uh, thanks." The words sound as soft as her hair looks and as guarded as her face.

I nod and head past her, leaving her to her hot dog and her troubles.

I yank open a cooler and grab two sweet teas in one hand and the phone buzzing my pocket with the other.

"Fuckin' Tiny," I mutter.

Tiny's been like a damn housemother since we bought the property. I scan the text just to confirm it's from him and pocket my phone. Tiny can wait.

I grab a bottle of water to add to the teas and head for the register.

"I'm so sorry, I…" The little bird in the yoga pants is already being checked out. There is a hot dog on the counter along with some other snacks, and Mr. Green Glitter Eye Shadow is shaking his head.

"Lady, card's declined. Won't go through. I ran it three times." He drops the piece of plastic on the counter. "You got cash?"

I stand a respectful distance behind her, trying not to look at her ass in those yoga pants. I look anywhere but down, aiming for her sunshine hair and the sleeveless tank that reveals trim, almost muscular arms.

She's telling the attendant her card worked fine when she paid for gas outside at the pump. "Could you try it again? Please?" she asks, her voice proud, but the exhaustion of defeat sneaks through.

The kid huffs a sigh, but he picks up the card and runs it again. After a second, he raises his brows. "Okay? Satisfied?" he asks. He hands it back to her. "Won't go through. I'm sorry, all right? It's shitty, but this isn't our fault. You gotta pay cash or…"

My eyes trace what look like finger-shaped bruises on the backs of her upper arms. The marks aren't faint, but they are starting to heal. They look recent enough that I'm sure, goddamned sure, that somebody gripped her and shook her not that long ago. Shook her hard.

She drops her head in her hands. I stare past her to the shit she has piled on the counter. A hot dog loaded with ketchup. Two bags of chips. One water, one juice.

I pull out my money clip and peel off a $50.

"Here's your cash," I say to the attendant, reaching past her.

The woman faces me, her expression unreadable.

"Better not to use the card readers at the pump," I say. I'm trying to save her pride here, and by the looks on everyone's faces, we all know it. "You know those things all have skimmers on them," I explain.

"Skimmers?" she echoes, like she has no clue.

"Scammers steal card numbers from gas pumps all the time," I say. I point to her card, which she's now clutching tight in her hand. "Maybe check with your bank, maybe there's been some kind of fraud. There's usually a reason why these things don't work when they should."

The attendant holds up a hand with the change, looking unsure who to give it to.

"That's his," she says quietly. She blinks at me, but she doesn't say thanks or anything.

I pay for my water and teas with the change and nod to the gas station dude. "Thanks, man," I say and grab my stuff.

"Need a bag for that?" the kid asks.

"Not me," I say. I instinctively breathe deeply, hoping to catch a hint of that sugar-cookie fragrance before I head toward the door.

"Wait!"

I stop at my bike and face the woman calling after me.

"You didn't have to do that," she says. She's got the hot dog in one hand and her snacks in one of those cheap white plastic sacks imprinted with the words Thank You. The words repeat over and over in a pattern that seems excessively enthusiastic given the fact that the bags hold crappy gas-station chips.

I slide my sunglasses over my eyes. "Forget it," I say, lifting my chin at her. Now that she's facing me, staring me down, I can tell she's not all baby bird. She's got strength in her eyes and something else I can't place. Fierceness, maybe. Whatever it is, none of this is my problem. "It's kinda my fault," I say, making light of it. "I really pushed you toward that dog. I hope you enjoy it."

She smiles at that but then flicks a glance over toward a beat-up sedan parked in the shade at one of the pumps. She quickly looks back at me, but I'm thinking that must be her car.

"Look, I...I want to pay you back," she says. "Can you wait here a second?"

I sigh and watch as she dashes to the car. I don't even try to keep my eyes off her juicy ass as she runs.

Her hair flicks against her back with every step, and before I know it, she's walked around one side and opens the rear passenger door. She looks up at me, watching me watching her, and I see her pass the hot dog to someone in the back seat.

I strain my eyes to make out…a kid.

A little girl.

She hands the hot dog and plastic bag to the little girl, talks to her for a moment—all the while keeping one eye on me—and then trots back across the gas station lot back to me and my bike.

She holds out a crumpled five-dollar bill and has her cell in her hands. "I only have a little cash on me," she explains. "But I'd like your number or address so I can mail you a check when I get…"

The heavy pause lets me know that this little bird is flying away. Either doesn't know where she's headed or doesn't want to say.

"When you get…?" I repeat, saying it like a question.

Her sudden silence reveals the truth. A woman with bruises on her arms and no cash. Beat-up car and shifty eyes. A little girl in the back, eating cheap-ass food at a rest stop.

I hold out a hand. "Unlock your phone."

She swipes the touchscreen and punches in a code. Never taking her eyes off mine, she holds the phone out to me. I put my number in her contacts and hand the phone back.

But I can't leave this woman just yet. I look her over. The soft lines in her forehead I can now see are worry lines. The distrusting eyes. Perpetual look of concern. A woman and a little girl in a beater car with a single hot dog between them. I shake my head. "You wanna pay me back, my number is in there under Morris."

"Did you send my number to your phone?" she asks.

I shake my head. "You want to reach out, you can. I'm in there. But if you want to put this day in the rearview…consider the lunch a gift."

She looks at me confused, an upset-looking pucker twisting her pretty lips downward. "Why?" she asks. "Why are you doing this? I can't accept your generosity. I can't—"

"Did you fill your tank?" I ask pointedly. I didn't actually see her put her card into that pump, so I don't know if she has gas to get wherever she's going or not.

She gives me a sad look and a wry smile. Like I caught her. "I put some gas in," she admits.

"Some gas," I echo. I shake my head and dig into my pocket. I flick a glance around to make sure no one is watching us and then peel off two hundred in cash.

She sees the money, and her eyes widen. "What? What is this? What do you think you're doing?" She shakes her head and starts to back away.

Before she can get away, I reach out and grab her arm but gently. I lower my face and whisper in her ear, "I see those fucking bruises on your arms," I hiss. "I know the guy who grabbed you exactly like I'm doing right now didn't give you cash to go with those bruises. Only a dickless piece of shit would send his woman and kid—or a woman with a kid, whether it's his or not—away without a decent ride and money to get where they are going. I'm not a dickless piece of shit."

She struggles a little against my hold, but not in a way that makes me think she's scared. If I didn't know better, I'd think she was actually leaning closer.

"I'll keep out of your business after this. The two hundred means nothing to me. I've got ink worth more than that covering just my left thumb." I trace the line of her chin with my hand to prove the point. "I won't stand by and watch a woman and an innocent kid suffer when a couple bucks might see you safely home—or wherever you're going."

I release her and kick a leg over the seat of my bike. While this woman smells like an angel and looks like she was made for sin, I've got places to be. "Hey," I say, firing up my bike. "You need a job, a place to stay, or anything—you have my number."

She looks at her phone, reading the contact information I entered. "Morris?" she asks. "Your name is Morris, right?"

I nod. "That's me, darlin'."

She looks over my bike and my leather vest. Her eyes grow dark when she scans my chest, my neck, and finally, come to meet my eyes.

"Don't you want to know my name?" she asks. Her mouth is slightly open. I can almost taste the sugar-sweet air she puffs between those perfect lips.

I shake my head and give her a sexy smile. "You can tell me your name when you call me."

And with that, I take off, leaving my beautiful bird and her little chick behind.

CHAPTER
TWO
ALICE

I SUCK at this stealth shit.

I climb in the front seat of the car, and the first thing I do is check on my baby.

"Zoey, honey," I say, turning to face my daughter. "How was the hot dog? Do you want to go inside and use the bathroom?"

Zoey has a little ketchup on her chin, and when she nods, I reach between the driver's and passenger's seat to wipe at her face with a napkin. So much for keeping a low profile. I'd left her in the car so I could check out the gas station, scope out the bathroom, and make sure there weren't too many people around. I can't—won't—be too careful.

Alice Sparrow. Mother. Unemployed waitress. Soon-to-be total failure as a runaway.

"Yeah, Mommy. And I want to wash my hands. I got all sticky." Zoey unfastens her seat belt and scoots forward to climb out of her car seat. She's six, but she's small enough that she'll need that booster seat in the car for probably at least another couple years. But this isn't *her* booster seat. The nice one with high-tech performance fabric that wipes clean of crumbs and, well, ketchup. The one with roomy side compartments to hold juice cups and toys safely within reach and a nicely padded neck rest for long road trips.

Zoey is sitting in a broken-down, used booster seat. No cupholder, no performance fabrics, and no secret compartments to hold tiny toy parts and shoes. I picked this one up from a thrift store last week. Paid cash—I actually had cash back then. No receipt. No registration or warranty. It's not one she'll be using for long, but we needed something for the drive.

I'll buy her a replacement, a new one, as soon as I can. There's so much I'll need to replace, to give her. For now, her real seat is still back in my SUV, parked at the airport's long-term parking lot. Where, God willing, no one is looking for it. Or us. At least not yet.

"Come on, then, sweetie," I say, climbing out of the car. "I'll take you."

Before I help Zoey out of the car, I pull her baby-blue princess-themed baseball cap over her hair and tuck her braid through the adjustable plastic clip at the back that fits the cap to her head. I thought a lot about every detail of this plan in the months before we executed it. But our hair was something I struggled with. In the movies, women on the run always change their hair color. I finger the ends of my distinctive blond hair just thinking about it.

Maybe it's vanity. Maybe it's pure foolishness to think that we should be able to leave, to get away, without fundamentally hiding who we are. But eventually, the decision was made for me. With all the other logistics, I ran out of time to color our hair before we hit the road. So, for now, we both still have our distinctive honey-blond hair. Recognizable, yes, but that was a risk I knew we'd face no matter what. That's the risk we took by leaving. And yet, here we are. On the road, on the run, and it's way too late to change now.

I grip Zoey's hand and lock the car door behind us. We walk back into the gas station, and I avoid the eyes of the smug cashier. I walk straight to the bathroom, yank open the door, and wait inside with her while she goes.

I open my phone and look through my contacts. With a few quick strokes, I change Morris's name to Mary Morris.

I smirk, thinking back on the man. Who uses one name like a celebrity? Bikers, I suppose. If the big-ass motorcycle, the enormous muscles, and arms loaded with tats didn't give him away, the logo embroidered on the back of his black leather vest didn't leave much room for interpretation.

A biker. Go figure.

The good guys never look like heroes, but the villains somehow always do. A lesson almost every woman I know learned the hard way. I run my hands over my upper arms, the skin where he held me still warm from the firm, but gentle, pressure.

That's the difference between a man like Morris and an asshole like my husband, Jerry Cruz. Morris seems like the type who understands the difference between pressure and pain. If a guy like Cruz ever knew, he doesn't give a fuck anymore. A man like that chooses to inflict hurt. And is good at it.

"Mommy, there's not much soap." Zoey looks up at me for help. She presses the soap dispenser, and it sputters a tiny speck of blue liquid onto the dried soap splatters already coating the sink.

"It's okay, baby." I dig in my tiny teal bag for hand sanitizer and squirt a nice dollop onto her hands. "Just rub that really good and then rinse it off with water. We'll wash up when we get settled."

I swipe my phone to close the contacts. Just having Mary Morris in my phone makes my heart beat a little faster. Which is straight-up crazy. There is no way Cruz will find us. But just knowing that another man's number is in my phone... And one with kind eyes and a seductive grin. I shake my head to rid myself of thoughts of anyone but Cruz. There is only room for one man in my universe. And until I know he can never, ever get at my daughter and me again, I need to keep my eyes focused on one goal—escape.

Zoey uses the air dryer to dry her hands while I wad up a fistful of clean toilet paper to pull open the bathroom door.

I lead ZoZo back to the car, my head down, eyes darting around to make sure there are no familiar cars or faces among the few customers now filling their cars at the pumps.

I see a black SUV parked behind my car, and my breath catches in my chest. Without meaning to, I slam to a halt in place, jerking Zoey's hand in the process.

"Mommy?" she asks, not hurt but startled. "What is it? Is it Daddy Jerry?"

I flutter my eyes closed and fight back a wave of nausea. "You don't have to call him Daddy anymore, honey. You never need to say his name again, baby. He's never been your real dad, you know that."

I see an older woman dressed in bright tennis clothes slowly climb out of the SUV, and I breathe a little easier. Unless Cruz has hired a staff of lady enforcers, my anxiety can relax.

"Come on, honey." I duck my head and drag my baby back to the car. I settle Zoey in her booster seat, making sure she can reach whatever she might need while I'm driving.

"Your juice is here if you need it, okay?" I point to where I tucked the bottle snugly between the booster seat and the seat cushion. "But try not to sip it while the car is moving, okay?" I remind her, poking her belly and giving her a grin. "Remember…"

"Mommy!" Zoey covers her face with her hands in exasperation. "I was *four*!" She giggles hysterically as she remembers what I like to call "The Orange Juice Incident."

I shrug and try to keep the mood light. Even a couple minutes of laughter is a welcome departure from the stress of the morning. "I don't know, Zo," I tease, "I think I saw you looking really thirsty back there when we were speeding along the highway. I wouldn't want your special vacation dress to get a juice bath."

Zoey gives me that too-mature, too-knowing look she has when she knows I'm pulling her leg, and I climb into the front seat, lock the doors, and pull the paper map from the glove box. I have been so, so careful. For weeks, I've been planning how to give Zoey and me enough lead time to get far enough away from Jerry Cruz, so that when he does realize we're not just gone, but that I've left him, he'll have no fucking clue where to start.

I disabled the "find my phone" function from my smartphone and mapped out routes the old-fashioned way. Using paper maps. I resisted the urge to ever map the route on my phone. The damn thing was in Jerry's name. Who knows what information he could access once he knew to look?

Getting a new phone was the last thing I'd do on

my list, what I planned to do first thing tomorrow. When Jerry would expect me to wake up and call to check in from my sister's in Denver, I'd planned to be backing up over my phone with this stupid used car. But if the money situation isn't sorted out, that could mean a major problem. Keeping this phone means keeping one very clear path between Jerry and me open. And I intend to set fire to that path and never, ever look back.

In the meantime, I'm sticking with my old-school escape route. I check my notes, fold the map back up, and start the car, heading east toward the coast.

"Can I pick the music?" Zoey asks, squinting at the sunshine beaming through the windows.

"Yeah, baby, but only what's on the radio."

One of the only lies I've ever told my daughter, I told her this morning. The first was that Jerry Cruz, Zo, and I would be a forever family. But I sure as hell believed that to be true when I married that man two years ago. The second lie was this morning. She'd packed her iPad for the spring break trip everyone thought we were taking to visit my sister in Colorado. We loaded our suitcases into the car, our overnight bags, and Zoey held her iPad in her hands while we kissed Cruz goodbye.

"Call me when you land," he said. He held me by the upper arms, his favorite way to keep me close, to limit my ability to move out of his constant orbit. "Alice," he said, using my name like a curse. His fingers bit into my flesh, hard enough to

make me suck in a breath but not hard enough to draw Zoey's attention. "Don't forget me while you're with your sister. You know I don't like when you're away."

I swallowed hard and leaned forward, pouring every ounce of fake affection I could muster into my voice. "Baby," I crooned, "you know I hate being away from you. But a little spring break visit to her auntie will be good for Zoey. I'll call you constantly."

"Make sure that you do," he said. He kissed me, still holding fast to my arms. Then he turned his attention to my daughter. "Zoey, come here," he demanded.

The coffee soured in my stomach as I watched my daughter walk up to him, clutching her iPad in her hands.

"Yes, Daddy?" she said, like the well-trained seal he wanted her to be.

"I know you're not going to like Colorado much," he said, kneeling to meet her at eye level. He glanced at me, sending me an unspoken message with the ice in his eyes. "If you get bored, or if your aunt Rayne starts saying anything you think is wrong, you come right home. We live in the most beautiful state in the country, and you're going off to goddamn Denver for spring break."

I cringed. Not at his cursing, but at his not-so-subtle attempts to plant ideas in Zoey's head. He didn't want us to visit my sister. Didn't want us more than an arm's reach away. He didn't like when I talked to Rayne, didn't like, didn't want, didn't everything.

It was Jerry Cruz's way, or no way at all. And this was the classic Cruz maneuver. Infiltrate someone's thoughts and *opinions by planting his own in a way that seemed so reasonable, so normal, only a crazy person would think he was anything but a dedicated, caring man. After two years married to Jerry Cruz and resisting his attempts at gaining absolute control over my every thought and belief, I felt like a bona fide, stark raving lunatic. It took everything in me not to yank my daughter from his clutches and run right then.*

"Okay, Daddy. I'll miss you." Zoey repeated what she knew she was expected to say, her voice flat and her eyes dull. My heart caught. She was like a little robot with him. Well-trained. Knowing her place.

"See that?" He grinned, pulling little Zoey into a hug. "She already misses her daddy." He released my daughter and stepped close to me. "It's not too late, Alice," he hissed against my ear. "I can book you and Zoey a mommy-daughter spa day, you can go to the beach. There's no reason to go to Denver for spring break, is there? To go so far from home…"

"But Auntie Rayne got a puppy!" Zoey exclaimed, for a moment, the little girl in her forgetting that she wasn't supposed to interrupt the adults.

Jerry clenched his jaw and grabbed my arm again, tighter this time. "Alice," he warned.

"Zoey, honey," I said, more earnest than ever for her to listen, for her to meet Cruz's every expectation to the letter. At least for one more hour. One more hour. "Please don't interrupt Daddy Jerry, okay? Please apologize for being rude."

Zoey looked near tears, but she nodded. "I'm sorry, Daddy, but…"

"Zoey." His bark was so sudden and so loud, Zoey

flinched as though she'd been hit. She looked down at the new powder-blue tennis shoes we'd bought to wear on our special spring break trip. They matched the princess dress and baseball cap.

I swallowed hard, and Zoey stifled any sounds. She hung her head, and I could see the defeat sagging her shoulders.

At six, she already knew what it meant to be controlled. To give in. To bend her natural instincts to the will of someone stronger and more powerful. But all that was about to end.

"We need to load up the car!" I reminded her, putting on my most cheerful voice. Jerry still held my arm in a vise-like grip. I turned to him and gave him a sweet, sultry smile. "She's not behaving because of all the excitement. She's really excited to go on a plane, Jerry. I'll talk to her," I promised.

He looked at me with disgust. "I wonder if canceling the trip would teach her a lesson," he said.

Although my heart raced so hard I was sure Jerry could feel my pulse through my arm, I composed my face to stay calm.

He couldn't.

We couldn't cancel.

This was our only way out. Months of planning would be down the drain.

"I'll deal with it, sweetheart," I said, the endearment tasting like shit on my tongue. "Let's not cause a stir with my sister or anyone outside the family." While Jerry normally didn't give a damn what anyone else thought about what he did, he did know that canceling on my sister—whom I hadn't seen but two times since Jerry and I were married—would cause some concerns.

Maybe prompt her to visit us here in Florida. And he definitely did not want that.

"*We'll check in with you in a few hours, and we'll be back before you know it,*" I reassured him.

He released my arm but put a hand behind my neck and pulled me roughly to his face. The kiss he gave me wasn't one of love or lust. Jerry was the only man I'd ever met who could convey hatred with his lips.

"Mom!"

I jerk my head and meet Zoey's eyes in the rearview mirror, my memories of the morning shattering with the sound of the voice that gives my life purpose. "What, baby? What is it?"

She raises her cute little eyebrows at me. "You said I could pick the music."

I huff a sigh of relief.

Right. That.

I flick on the radio and fiddle with the stations until we find a pop station that will hopefully have mostly kid-friendly music. It's been so long since I played any music other than a custom streaming playlist, I have no idea what to expect from music on the radio.

After we said our goodbyes to Jerry and packed up the SUV, we drove to long-term parking at the airport, while Jerry headed off to work.

We parked the SUV beside a beat-up sedan that I'd purchased in cash only two days before. I quickly loaded Zoey into the beater, strapping her into the used booster seat. I opened up our beautiful new suitcases, which were in the back of the SUV. I transferred half the clothes and toiletries from our overly full bags into empty thrift store bags I'd stashed in the trunk of the sedan.

Then I left our nice luggage in the back of the SUV, left Zoey's booster chair right where it always was, strapped in behind the passenger seat, and turned her iPad completely off. I tossed the device underneath the driver's seat of the SUV, so no one would see it from outside the car and break in just to steal the iPad. In a couple days, the battery on the tablet would be dead, and there would be no way to pick up a signal or trace it. By the time Jerry realized we weren't in Denver and we weren't coming home, our abandoned car, half-empty luggage, and dead tablet would be all he had left.

But that meant Zoey had to give up her beloved iPad. I'd told her I'd accidentally forgotten it in the SUV and that I'd get her a new one as soon as I could. That was a lie, but it was the only way I could separate her from another device Jerry might use to track our location.

That was the second lie I'd ever told my daughter.

I hope it's the last.

Zoey seems content with the music, and I flick on a turn signal and roll the windows completely closed so I can crank the AC. Based on the notes I made and the map, we are less than an hour's drive from

Daytona Beach. If we're lucky, we'll find a small, safe motel. Whether they'll be able to take my fucked-up debit card or not is another worry.

I used a computer at the library to open a new bank account online using a PO box I paid for with cash.

I timed everything just right—I wasn't leaving anything to luck. The debit card arrived just a few days before Zoey's spring break was scheduled to start.

There would be no way Jerry could trace that account to me, but now I can see all that planning might not have stopped me from making a big mistake. Opening the account using some virtual bank that doesn't have real ATMs means the little money I do have is only accessible through a debit card that apparently isn't working.

I'll add that to the unexpected shit I'll need to sort out when we make it to Daytona.

At least with Morris's money, I should be able to find a cheap place to stay that I can pay for with cash, even if it's only for a night or two.

Two hundred bucks won't go far, but if the motel has internet, I should be able to contact the online bank and see if I can get at what little additional cash I have.

Hopefully in a couple days, I can find a job. Get Zoey into school.

To be honest, I didn't plan much past getting

away. So much effort went into making sure we had at least a couple days' lead time while Jerry thought we were in Denver with my sister… But I'm going to have to figure out what happens next fast.

As the sun raises the temperature in the car, I watch little Zoey's eyes drift closed. The traffic ahead is heavy, but nothing I can't navigate. I am just feeling my shoulders relax, my hands light on the steering wheel, when my phone starts buzzing. An immediate, panicked sweat breaks out on my lip.

That ringtone. It's Jerry.

How?! Why is he calling me? I pick up the phone and stare at it. Based on the time, we should be on a flight to Denver right now.

Why the hell would Jerry be calling?

No, no, no, fuck!

I nearly slam my foot on the brake and pull the car over, but I know I can't answer that call. I fight the instinct to respond to him immediately and will myself to think. Maybe he is calling to leave a message, reminding me to check in as soon as I land.

Anything could have happened, or nothing could have happened. That's how it is with Jerry. I can never predict when he'll ignore me for an entire day or get a bug up his butt and want to hear from me every hour on the hour. Calls, texts, insisting that I be in nearly constant contact. I'll know soon enough which this is, but right now, I need to get moving.

I put the pedal to the metal and start driving faster

on the highway. My heart rate is just starting to slow about ten minutes later, when a horrible thumping starts coming from under the hood of the car. It sounds like something broke loose and is rattling free in there, but before I can think what to do, the temperature gauge starts going wild on the dash, the small orange dial waving frantically to get my attention.

I try not to go into a full, losing-my-shit panic.

"Mommy? What's that?" Zoey is wide awake now, her hands over her ears to block out the noise.

"Don't worry, baby. It's just the car. It's acting up a bit."

The knocking noise gets worse until, finally, the entire car starts shaking in this back-and-forth, jerking motion that I can't drive through.

"Goddammit," I mutter.

I flip on my signal and lurch onto the shoulder just as the car sputters and dies.

And then it's official.

I can't help it. I go into a full-blown panic.

I try to turn the engine over, start the car again, but every time I turn the key in the ignition, I hear a click-click-click, and then nothing.

Dead.

The only means of escape I have is dead. Just like I'm going to be.

It's blazing hot outside, and we're pulled over on the left-hand side of the road, cars in the fast lane speeding past us at over seventy miles an hour. I feel like a sitting duck, and I'm stranded with a helpless little duckling.

I race to think of options, but my phone is lighting up again, Jerry's fucking number on the caller ID.

"Mommy?" Zoey asks in a small voice from the back seat. "What is it?"

I open my purse and tear through my wallet, wishing I had everything I had back home. Roadside assistance. A reliable SUV. Credit cards with high credit limits. But none of those things were *mine*. Everything in my world belonged to Jerry Cruz. My, for now, husband. Everything except this shitty sedan, some used luggage, and my baby girl.

I swallow hard and rub my eyes before turning to reassure Zoey. But before I can even twist in my seat, a heart-wrenching cry tears from the back seat.

"Mama!" Zoey cries, fat tears rolling down her face. "Mama, I'm sorry!"

I frantically scan the back seat, braced for blood or vomit or worse. Thankfully, it's not worse. But it's not great. Zoey is holding an empty plastic bottle of apple juice in her hand. The entire contents of the bottle have spilled down the front of her baby-blue princess dress.

"I'm not a baby. It was an accident," she says, coughing through her tears. "I'm sorry, Mama. I'm sorry!"

Her overreaction to a small but inconvenient spill

tears at my heart. No little girl should feel full-body shame over fucking apple juice and a wet dress.

Fuck this. Fuck Jerry. This reaction is all him. This is what years of living with Jerry have done to my daughter. To me.

I am stranded on the side of a six-lane road in a junk-ass car with two hundred dollars in cash from a stranger.

This is not how my life was supposed to go.

"Zoey," I say in a firm voice, facing my daughter. "Don't cry, sweetheart." I try to hold my voice steady. "It's okay. You're okay. Everything is okay."

But even as I say the words, something inside me shrivels. I just told my daughter lie three.

Everything is *not* okay.

CHAPTER
THREE
MORRIS

I ROLL up to the property and park my bike out front. There is a paved parking lot, but it's in atrocious condition. The pockmarks in the concrete are so deep it looks like a hoard of wild boars wearing steel spikes on their feet stampeded through, not once but twice. The fractures in the walkways are large enough to trip a person and cause some serious injuries.

This place is a *total* piece of shit, but it's ours.

There are at least four separate storefronts that I can count, but every one of them is completely boarded up. There's minimal graffiti on the plywood, which is good.

Means I won't have to fight local shitheads to keep them off the property. But securing the place while we rebuild is going to be an issue.

As I walk up to one of the shops and peer in the

windows, I guess that anything of value has long been looted. Probably by the former owner, but still.

From what I can see through the small gaps between the plywood planks, the interiors have been stripped bare. The roof looks as if a family of raccoons has built a compound up there. What grounds there are haven't been mowed or weeded in… Shit. The nearly two acres as far as the eye can see is basically feral.

"*Fuuuuuck.*"

I should have driven my truck here today. I don't have tools with me, and without breaking down some of what's boarded up, I'm going to have to bust a window or door to access the building.

The bank agent handed me a single key at closing. *A single key.* Even figuring out which door that key opens—because there's no way that one key unlocks all these shops—is going to take some time.

I peer in the windows and try every door handle with the key, but they are all a no-go. Since it looks like I'm not getting in clean, I may as well go dirty.

I scan the ground for a brick, a rock, or any concrete debris I can use to bust my way into a window or pry off a bit of plywood, when I hear the sound of an engine turning over or trying to.

The noise is coming from behind the building. I haven't even gone back there yet, but there are no neighbors or other businesses, so whoever is back there…is probably fucking stealing.

"Goddamn it," I mutter.

I head around the side of the building and keep my steps quiet. My fists have gotten me into and out of trouble more times than I can count, but if whoever is on the other side of this building is packing, it sure as fuck won't be a fair fight.

Once I'm on the side of the building, I can see a huge extended cab black pickup with a small flatbed trailer hitched on the back. There is an antique, beat-to-shit yellow Ford Bronco half-cab parked near the flatbed.

I'm assuming the piece-of-shit truck doesn't run because there is somebody behind the wheel of the classic truck who looks focused on trying to get the engine to turn over.

I come up quietly around the Bronco from behind. The windows on the half-cab are either broken or rolled down, but I have a clear reach in if I'm quick.

I scan the pickup, the trailer, and the entire scene. There's only this one guy as far as I can tell, but I'm not taking any chances. I see my shot and rush the truck.

"Hey, asshole!" I pound on the driver's side door once with my fist, then reach through the open window and grab the shirt of the guy inside.

"What the fuck!" The kid puts his hands up like he's surrounded by the cops, which is actually what I want. No gun or other weapon that I can see, so for the moment, I've got the upper hand.

I yank open the driver's side door, tighten my fist around the guy's work shirt, and physically drag his ass out of the truck. Not willing to take any chances, I release the guy only long enough to make a fist and aim for his gut. I land a single punch that knocks him to the ground, where he rolls around, gripping his stomach and sputtering a cough.

"Fuck!" he groans, settling over on his side and panting.

"You packin'?" I demand, standing over him, my steel-toe boot lined up to his balls. I like a fair fight, but I'm not above kicking a man when he's down if it means not getting my face blown off. "You got a weapon? Anybody else here?"

The kid tries to stand, but he gives up and rolls over onto his back, covering his face with his hands. "Jesus, fuck," he sputters. He coughs weakly, but I know he's gonna be fine in a couple seconds.

"Unless you want this—" I nudge the tip of my boot into the broken asphalt. "I'd start talking if I were you."

The kid holds his hands up and looks me in the eye. He can't be more than twenty-five, if that. He's wearing a work shirt and jeans. "I'm alone," he assures me. "I don't even own a gun. I got nothing. Jesus!"

I watch him closely as, one hand still up, his eyes

never leaving mine, he struggles to stand. He holds his gut and bends slightly, huffing a breath, but before I know what's coming, he tackles me to the ground and starts pummeling the shit out of my face.

"You punk-ass motherfucker!"

Goddamn this kid.

We tussle on the ground, but it's not long before I've got my full weight on him.

"Who are you?" I ask calmly, giving us both a chance to catch our breath. Getting into a fight in the midmorning sun is the last thing I wanted to do this morning. "Why the fuck are you here?"

"Leo," he grunts. "Leo Hawk."

"And why the fuck are you stealing, Leo?"

"Come on, man," he says. "Let me up. I can explain."

"I can hear you just fine," I say. "Go 'head. Why are you trying to steal my shit?"

Leo jerks his body, trying to free himself. But that ain't happening. I'm 265 pounds of solid muscle, and despite the more than twenty years I probably have on this kid in age, I'm on top of this situation…literally.

I use my left hand to grab the back of his collar and give him another shake, making sure the asphalt pebbles on the ground give his face a couple of contact kisses.

"Fuck!" he yells.

"Don't be a pussy," I scold. "I've had hickeys that left deeper marks than that. Now, why don't you stop crying and start talking? I might just let you leave my property with most of your face intact."

"Okay, okay."

I feel his body relax a little.

It's resignation. Maybe defeat.

"Hawk Enterprises," he explains. "That was my brother."

"Why do I know that name?"

"He owned this whole strip. And then fucking lost it. He's an addict. He shot all the profits into his arm or spent it on strippers. Jesus, I don't know."

The kid sounds miserable, broken enough that I want to believe him. Liars don't usually sound so shredded.

"You're the one who looted the property?"

"I wouldn't say looted, man," Leo says. "This building was all we had. Our parents are dead. It's just me and Tim. He's older. Always been handy. We both are. There's nothing mechanical we can't fix. I've worked with him here in the restoration bays doing auto repair since I was eighteen. Last seven years of my life. I didn't know my brother wasn't paying the mortgage. I found out the bank put the place up for sale when I came to work one day and the sheriff had pasted a notice on the door. Everything we've worked for, everything we know. Fuckin' gone."

"And the truck?"

Leo jerks his head to the side to try to meet my eyes. "That's mine, man. All mine. You can check the title. My grandfather left that truck to me when he passed. 1968 Ford Bronco half-cab." Leo cracks a small smile, pride evident in his tone. "Gramps always said my momma was made in that truck. Not cool, telling a teenage boy his mom was conceived in a classic half-cab, but it sure brought me some kind of luck when I drove it."

I have to laugh at that.

"I've been clearing out the building since the auction," he explained. "Little by little, I moved out the shit we'd accumulated in here. Tools and equipment. Anything I needed to try to survive once we lost this place. I moved all of it to my gramps' house. I live there now, and I thought at least I could try to start over on my own. Do some repairs out of my house, something."

"And the truck?" I ask again.

"The truck needs engine work. Hasn't run well for the last two years, but we never had the extra cash to buy the parts to bring it back to life. Tim kept promising me, but…"

The kid sighs, and I can hear the disappointment.

The resentment.

It always is the ones closest to you who fuck you with the sharpest sticks.

"I would have had it out of here last week. I didn't think I could drive it all the way home, so Tim promised to help me get it on the trailer, but you can guess how that went."

Just then, my phone starts ringing. It's not a ringtone I set up for any of the brothers. Without loosening my hold on the kid, I pull the phone from my pocket.

It's a number I don't recognize with a Miami area code.

I look at Leo and back at my phone and decide whatever it is can wait.

"You like bleeding?" I ask him. It's not a question. "If I let you up, you're gonna be cool, we clear? You try to fuck me…"

"I won't," Leo says in a rush. "Look, you yanked me out of my truck and punched me. I didn't know who the fuck you were."

"Well, now you do," I say, releasing my grip on his arm. "I'm the new owner of this property." I stand up. "And everything on it." Of course, after being down on the ground that long, my knee pops and cracks as I'm standing as if a firecracker went off. "This getting-old shit is for the goddamn birds," I say, shaking my leg to loosen the stiffness.

Leo looks at me like he's surprised I've got anything to say that's not a question or a threat. I obviously can't let the kid loot the property, but I respect what he was trying to do.

In the same position, I'd do exactly what he's doing. Although I probably would not have been quite so up front about it. In my younger years, I tended to punch first and ask questions later. Fuck, that still seems to be my MO.

I reach a hand out to the kid.

"Morris," I say.

Leo shakes my hand and nods, his lips a thin line, probably because of what I just said, the tiny reminder that that truck he was trying to load onto a flatbed was auctioned off along with everything else he'd stolen from me.

Just then, my phone buzzes with a text.

"Goddamn it!" I bark, pulling out my phone.

"You know, you can silence those alerts," the kid says, trying to be helpful.

I shoot him an impatient look. "Yeah, yeah. If I did that, I'd never get my calls and texts."

Leo looks like he's trying not to laugh at me, but the look I give him quickly wipes the amusement off his face.

"Wait here," I say. I swipe at the screen and see the same number, that same Miami area code, has now sent me a text.

Hi, Morris. It's me. From the gas station.

Well, look at that.

Little Miss Yoga Pants is burning up my phone line. A memory of her sugar-sweet smell and that sunshine hair makes my dick perk up and take notice. But then I realize it's been just barely an hour since I left her. Maybe she got where she was going and wanted to make sure she reached out to pay me back. Or maybe not.

A woman traveling alone with a kid and very little money can only mean one of two things. As much as my ego would like to think she's interested, I'm willing to bet something else is going on.

The little bird's in trouble.

"I gotta make a call," I tell Leo. "Should only take a minute. Stay right here, and we'll sort this shit out."

Leo nods and reaches a hand into his pocket.

"Hey!" I make a move to grab his hand.

"Dude, chill!" Leo points to his pocket. "My phone. I'm just going to check my phone. We're good, okay? God."

I nod and decide to trust him for the moment. I scroll to my missed calls and tap on the Miami number to dial her back.

"What's up, sweetheart?" I say in greeting. "Got your text."

"Morris…" The raw panic in her voice unnerves me. I can hear a little girl crying in the background and not much else.

"Hey, hey, hey. What the fuck happened? Where are you?"

I listen for a few minutes, fighting the animal instinct to jump on my bike and take off toward her. An unreasonable urge to snap something in half takes over as she explains.

"Stay where you are," I interrupt her suddenly. "Do you know where you are?"

She gives me the mile markers and some landmarks, as well as lets me know what direction she was traveling.

"Stay inside the car. Crack one of the doors facing away from the traffic if you need to let in more fresh air," I tell her. "You have water? Something to drink?"

She reassures me they are safe and have water.

"I'll be there as fast as I can," I tell her. "Anyone talks to you or tries to stop, you call me right back."

I end the call and look Leo over. He's got an older extended cab pickup truck and a flatbed trailer. I've got a bike and no helmets.

"You really a mechanic?" I ask, and he nods. "You any good?"

"Better than good." Leo lifts his chin.

"All right, then," I say. "How'd you like to work out a deal?"

CHAPTER
FOUR
ALICE

JERRY LEFT me three voice messages over the last hour. I know if I turn off my phone I won't have to see the calls coming in, but then I also won't be able to watch for a message or a call from Morris. He texted me that he was on his way with help, but I don't know what that means.

All I can do is wait.

And hope like hell Jerry is just having a needy day. Right now, I should be miles above the ground on an airplane. Phone off, shoes off, sipping a mimosa, while Zoey entertains herself with a movie on her iPad.

As far as Jerry knows, everything is as it should be.

"Mama," Zoey says, breaking my train of thought. She still looks sad and apologetic. "Do we have to go back home now? Because the car is broken, does that mean we can't take our adventure?"

I turn in the driver's seat to face her. "No, baby," I assure her. "You remember what I told you this morning? When I explained we aren't going to Auntie Rayne's?"

Zoey nods. "We're never going back home," she repeats what I told her.

"That's right," I say, trying to sound positive. Upbeat. Cheerful about the possibilities for the future, instead of terrified that one wrong move—like buying a shitty beater as a getaway car—could upend months of planning. "We're going to start over. Just me and you. No more angry Jerry, no more strict rules. Just me and you and a new start."

She stares out the window before looking at me, fresh tears in her eyes. "But, Mama…"

The look on her face makes me want to climb over the seat and hold her in my lap, kiss the fear away. "Yeah, baby? What is it?"

"Does that mean we're not going back for my iPad?"

I laugh out loud at that. "Sweetie, we're not going back for that old iPad. But I promise you, we're going to get you a brand-new one, okay? It will take us a little time, but the first special thing I buy when I get a new job will be an iPad."

"You're going to get a job?" Her eyes widen.

I haven't worked in years. Since Jerry and I got married, and he rescued me from the life of a single mom working as a waitress. Never enough money to cover babysitters, never enough sleep, never enough anything.

I would say it was a nice two years of comfort, but everything comes at a cost.

I know better now.

There really is no such thing as happily ever after.

"What are you gonna do?" Zoey asks. "Are you going to work at a car place like Dad—I mean like…"

I shake my head. "No, honey. Jerry works at an auto dealership."

He owns three, actually. Which is why the fact that I had to buy a beater from a used car lot to escape him is just about the best example of irony I can think of.

"I'm going to do something different, something fun."

"Like work at a carnival?" she asks, getting excited.

"No, baby. Not a carnival."

"Mommy, I'm hot." ZoZo wipes a hand on her face. Little beads of sweat gather on her upper lip.

"Come here, baby, have a sip of my water." I reach between the seats to hand her my water just as a beat-up–looking truck pulls out of traffic and parks behind me on the shoulder.

I breathe a sigh of relief.

Morris.

I can't believe he's here.

Part of me doesn't know what to say, what to do.

How to get out of the car and deepen the debt I owe to this man.

But then I get a look at the guy getting out of the car.

It's *not* Morris. This man is small, wiry, and he's looking my car over in a way that makes me feel instantly on edge. He's sizing us up.

My heart starts to race. "Zoey, stay in the car," I command. I can't roll the electric windows up, but I flip the fob as I get out to lock Zoey in the car.

I get out of the driver's door and step onto the gravel shoulder. I pull my sunglasses over my eyes so I can see the man through the glaring sunshine. I wave a hand at him, motioning as if to tell him to move away, not to come closer.

"We're all set here," I call out. "Thanks anyway."

He nods, indicating he's heard me, but he doesn't stop. He walks a little closer, never pulling his eyes from me until he ducks his head to peer inside the car.

Zoey has climbed out of her booster and is sitting in the back seat, peering at us through the open window.

I want to scream for her to get away from the window, but so far, the guy hasn't done anything to trigger my intense reaction. I don't want to make a situation that's not bad—at least not yet—turn that way.

"Broke down, huh?" he says, clearly ignoring what I just said.

"We're just fine," I tell him. "Just a little car trouble. My husband's on his way."

I lie on instinct because first, someone *is* on his way, and two, the way this skinny, shifty man is looking at my daughter is more than making the hairs on my neck stand on end. I feel sick with a worry that can only be described as fight-or-flight. I want to take a picture of his license plate and call the cops, scream for help…but there's no reason for that just yet.

Maybe too many years with Jerry have made me overly suspicious. I wasn't polite or even friendly with Morris, and he's a complete stranger on his way to help me.

There are good ones out there, I remind myself.

"Husband's not here now, though." He walks closer to the car, boldly meeting my eyes.

Then he doesn't say anything. He just stares like a hungry wolf deciding whether to kill or play with his prey. He's already past my bumper, which means Zoey is halfway between us.

"You need to leave," I say loudly. "We don't need your help. Just go."

"That's not very friendly of you," he says, flicking a glance toward the car. "Hot day. Your little girl shouldn't be locked inside that car. Why don't you bring her out here in the fresh air?"

I reach for my phone but realize I didn't grab it. In my rush to confront the man, I only grabbed the key fob. I clutch the car key in one hand and think fast. Traffic is flying past us, cars hazardously close.

If I stay beside the car and this fucker tries anything, cars passing by might not be able to see us, to witness anything.

If I walk backward, toward the front of the car, I'll be in the line of sight of drivers as they go by. I might be able to attract some attention waving for help. But doing that will put me farther away from him. And from Zoey.

"Listen, asshole!" I shout, trying another tactic. "You need to fucking leave! We don't want your help!"

The man tilts his head before lunging forward and jiggling the door handle.

Zoey lets out a scream, and I follow, lurching toward him.

Just then, an enormous black pickup truck screeches up behind us, parking behind the beat-up truck. Gravel dust is kicked up by the enormous tires, and through the cloud, I make out a familiar beard and neck tattoos. I can see my biker is in the passenger seat.

"Morris!" I scream.

I don't know who's driving, but right now, it could be Jerry himself behind the wheel for all I care.

The passenger door flies open, and Morris is walking toward me, his heavy boots hitting the pavement in time with my heartbeat. I immediately want to rush into his enormous arms, but I can see he's sizing up the situation.

"What's going on here, baby?" He is speaking to me but staring holes in the stranger. "We got a problem?"

Morris doesn't even have to try to look menacing. The sweet man who gave me advice about picking a hot dog could blister the paint off a wall with the look he's giving this strange man. Something in my chest catches.

Not fear, but pride.

He's doing this for me.

Protecting me.

Protecting us.

The stranger steps away from my car door and holds up his hands. "Just a good Samaritan stopping to help," he explains. "Looks like you've got this under control now."

He flits a glance back to me and then looks right through my car window, back at Zoey.

"It's a hot day for a little girl to be stuck in a car," he says, somehow making it sound like an explanation.

"Why don't you let me handle my business," Morris says, his tone menacing. He strides up to the man and raises his thick eyebrows in a challenge. "You wanna leave, or should I make it so you're the one who's stuck by the side of the road? Doing a lot less breathing?"

The thin man, calm as anything, presses his lips together and lowers his head. "I'll be on my way," he says. He scurries past Morris, climbs in his truck, and merges back into traffic.

As soon as the man is out of sight, I shove my sunglasses off my face. I take one long look at Morris and another at my little girl.

"Baby?" Morris asks. "You all right?"

I realize in that moment he still doesn't know my name.

But I don't care.

I walk up to him and throw myself against his chest.

CHAPTER FIVE

MORRIS

THE MOMENT I have my arms around her, I breathe in that sugar-sweet fragrance, and I feel it.

I feel her fear.

Her relief.

Her trust.

I hold her tight against me, the traffic noise rushing past, but for a few seconds, all I can do is see red.

Rage at this little bird getting stuck in the path of another predator.

What if I hadn't gotten here when I did?

Another ten, fifteen minutes, and who knows what kind of danger they would have been facing?

Even as I think it, I realize I've got it backward. This little bird can't fly free without being stalked.

Everywhere she goes.

Beautiful and vulnerable.

Not anymore.

Not if I can help it.

I watch the little girl's face that's pressed against the partially open window. I give her a reassuring smile and tighten my hold on her mama. Then I lean back so I can look into her eyes. "You're all right now," I assure her. "Did he do anything? You wanna call the cops?"

"No," she says quietly. "No. But he was... I was so..."

"It's all right," I say, shaking my head. The fact that she's safe is all I need to know. If I hear any more, I'm gonna take Leo's truck and haul ass after that motherfucker and use my bare hands to loosen his nuts. I don't need that kind of bloodshed on my hands, as satisfying as it would be. "Let's get you out of here," I say.

She doesn't move out of my arms, and as much as I love having her there, we have a child and a dead car to move, and it is getting hotter by the minute.

"Sweetheart?" I say again, trying to break through.

"Right...right." She sniffs hard and nods at me, stepping away from me. "God. Right, sorry. I just—"

"'S'all right," I say. "Leo!" I motion for the kid to get out of the truck. "Come here, come meet..."

I look at her and crack a grin. "A little help here, sweetheart?"

She looks at me in confusion until Leo ambles

over. He is taking in my little bird. I can feel him assessing her sunshine hair and caramel eyes. Just the thought of his eyes on her body makes me second-guess my decision to let him keep his pretty face.

"Leo, this is…"

"Alice," she says, stepping forward and extending her hand. She flicks me a sweet smile, knowing that she still hasn't told me her name. "I'm Alice Sparrow. Thank you so much for coming here to help."

Before the boy can get in a word, I grab his shoulders in a rough, tight hold.

It's meant to seem brotherly but to send a message at the same time.

"Alice," I say, liking the feel of her name on my tongue. Makes me want to taste everything about her. "Leo here is going to help get this car taken care of. He's going to keep his eyes—and everything else that he wants to keep attached to his body—to himself. Isn't that right, Leo?"

Alice flushes, and her sweet lips curve into a smile.

"I'm just here to help, ma'am," Leo says, and I immediately like the kid a lot better for his manners. He may not be a total dumbass after all.

I release him and wave at the little one in the car. "We're going to help your momma, sweetheart," I say.

Alice turns and unlocks the car door, and the little girl practically leaps from the back seat and into her mother's arms.

I can't believe Alice has the strength to carry the kid. She's like a full-grown child, not a baby, but despite Alice's tiny frame, she holds her daughter like I would if she were mine. Like she is everything.

"Morris, Leo," Alice says, "this is my daughter, Zoey."

Zoey rests her head on her mom's shoulder for a minute but then slides from her mom's arms to stand on these sparkly blue shoes. She holds a hand out to me first like a perfectly mature little person.

"Hello," she says. "Nice to meet you."

Her formal words feel rehearsed to me. Like someone's drilled into this kid what her place is. I kneel on the ground so I'm eye level with her.

"Hiya, Zoey." I look at her hand and then look to Alice for silent permission to shake Zoey's hand.

Something about their situation, the stranger they just had in their space, makes me want to be extra careful. I'm guessing I'm not exactly the kind of man she's used to shaking hands with, and she confirms that by staring with big, wide eyes at the ink tattooed up the backs of my hands.

"You ever see tattoos like this before?" I ask. I show her the backs of my hands. "It's just artwork, just pictures some people like to put on their bodies."

Zoey nods. "I draw with markers on my knees sometimes, but Da—" She stops herself and looks down. "I'm not supposed to do that."

Her little hand is still out for me to shake. Alice gives me a nod, so I take the little hand in mine.

"That's a good handshake," I say. "You're a strong young lady. With some pretty sparkly shoes."

Zoey pulls her hand back and immediately starts talking about the shoes.

"They're from this movie I love, I don't know if you've ever seen it, but it's all about these princess sisters—"

The words come out in a rush until she stops herself and slams her mouth shut, then takes a step back and hangs her head.

I look from the kid to Alice, confused. Alice's expression is dark, her face erased of its light.

"Yeah?" I urge. "You were saying? These princess sisters?"

I'm not following why she stopped talking until I look to Alice. She sets a hand on her daughter's shoulder.

"It's okay," Alice says. "Morris doesn't mind hearing about it. You can talk."

I snap my face toward Alice.

You can talk?

What kind of kid needs permission to talk? I'm no dad, never have been, but it seems like kids do and say what they want.

Normally getting them to stop talking is the problem.

The formal handshake and the self-restraint mean only one thing to me. She's been trained this way.

To keep her eyes down and her mouth closed. That seals it. Whoever this man is that Alice is running from, I fucking hate him.

Control.

That's what all this screams.

The shitty car, the lack of money, the barely there bruises a reminder and a warning.

The overly well-behaved little girl.

All the signs of control.

My desire to make meat stew out of this son of a bitch is just about bubbling over, when Leo calls out my name.

While I was chatting up Zoey about shoes, Leo popped the hood on Alice's sedan.

"Morris." The kid shakes his head. "We're going to need to tow it. I can't fix this without a repair bay and some parts."

I nod and stand to face Alice. "Where were you headed?" I ask. "You're gonna need a tow."

Alice swallows hard, and it's as if I can picture her doing the math in her head of how much a repair and a tow will cost.

"Don't worry about the money right now," I assure her. "One thing at a time. Where you headed?"

Alice's face again goes blank. I step close to her, breathing her in. I want to take a fistful of that hair and tug her back against my chest. Reassure her that this shit is nothing. A couple bucks and a little time. I got this. I got her.

"You can trust me," I say, trying to get past whatever walls she's got up. "I only want to help. No strings."

Alice rubs her face, and I can tell she believes me, even if she doesn't want to.

"Alice," I urge.

"We were going to get a motel room near Daytona," she admits. "Well, that was the plan. Short-term, at least."

"Short-term... You got an address?" I press. "We can drop you there."

Alice shakes her head. Her caramel eyes look sad, like I've cracked her code in just one move. "I didn't get that far," she says. "We...don't have a reservation."

Well, fuck.

"Leo," I call out. "Let's get the sedan on the trailer."

I turn to Alice. "You have what you need from the car?"

She shakes her head. "No, my phone and charger are in there. All our luggage. And the booster seat." She points at the back seat. "Zoey still needs to ride in a booster."

That's news to me. But all right. We got a plan.

"Pop the trunk for me, sweetheart."

I motion for Leo to help me move Alice's luggage

into the truck. She's giving Zoey instructions to stand right by the car and not to move while Alice leans into the open rear door and starts messing with the booster seat.

I can't help appreciating her long legs and that perfectly tight ass, but I tear my eyes away when I see Leo's fixed on the same thing I am.

Mine.

"Hey, kid."

"Yeah?" Leo comes up to me after loading the suitcases in the back of his truck.

I look at Alice and then Leo. Alice and then Leo.

"Let me make one thing clear," I say, slinging a heavy arm over the kid's shoulders. "Mine. Simple as that. You and me gotta sort out between us what's yours and what's mine, but this—" I nod toward Alice, who's struggling to pull the booster chair from the back seat "—is mine. Unless you want your nutsac hanging from the tailpipe of my bike."

Leo nods, a fast, curt move. "Got it, loud and clear. I got it," he says.

"Good." I motion for him to grab the kiddie seat from Alice. "Now figure out what the hell we do with that thing so we can get the fuck outta here. Then we got some things of yours to talk about."

CHAPTER
SIX
ALICE

BY THE TIME Leo and Morris get my car onto the trailer, all the luggage moved over, and the booster seat set up, all of us are drenched with sweat.

I am braced for things to turn on a dime.

For Morris to turn from the passenger seat of the pickup, glare at me, and unleash a fury of blame.

This is my fault.

I did this.

I deserve to fail.

I deserve to be alone, broke, and abandoned.

I'm braced for the shift in him, and I can already hear his voice—some voice—echoing in my head with all that and worse.

But as I belt Zoey into the seat and strap myself in beside her, Morris turns and pulls a red bandanna from his vest pocket.

"Sweet motherf…" He looks at Zoey and widens

his eyes. He redirects quickly. "Of princesses. Mother of princesses." He stammers, trying to veer away from cursing.

Leo shakes his head from the driver's seat, no doubt holding back laughter. I'm having a hard time believing what I'm hearing.

He holds out the bandanna to me. "Last chance," he says, his cheeks ruddy from the heat. "I've only got one of these, and I'm the sweatiest mother...of princesses...I'm the sweatiest mother of princesses in this truck. You wanna towel off first?"

I look him over curiously. "But then that'll be all sweaty for you."

"Sugar, I don't mind it sweaty." Morris waggles his eyebrows at me, and I feel my cheeks heat.

Leo chortles and meets my eyes in the rearview mirror. "I've got AC." He fires up the truck, rolls the windows up tight, and blasts the vents.

"You go ahead," I say to Morris. "We're okay." I open my purse and grab some tissues from a tiny travel pack and blot my face and neck.

Zoey's cheeks are pink, so I urge her to drink a little water.

"Where are we going?" I ask, half not wanting to know. It's completely insane, not to mention reckless, to have climbed in the car of a total stranger.

To have no place to go.

No way to get there.

As I worry through my many poor choices, my phone buzzes with an incoming call.

Jerry's number flashes on my caller ID, and I quickly silence the phone. I stuff the phone back into my purse and put the wadded-up tissues in with it.

Morris seems to register my concern, but his eyes narrow only briefly before he turns to face forward and mops his neck with the bandanna. "I have a place," he says. "Apartment. Don't stay there much. But it's safe and quiet. I'll bring you and Princess Zoey there until we can get wheels back under you."

I suck in a breath of the icy air that's finally streaming toward the back seat of the truck. "Where do you stay if you don't stay at your place?" I ask.

As soon as the words are out, I regret them. He's probably got a girlfriend.

Of course, a man like this, a powerful, kind man, doesn't sleep alone at home every night.

I don't even know him, but I realize I really don't want to hear the answer to the question I just asked. But then Morris surprises me.

"I got a room at the compound," he says. "I'm VP, so I spend most nights in my room over there anyway, shooting the shi—" He flicks a glance behind him at Zoey. "Shooting the poop, playing cards. You know. That kind of thing."

"Compound?" I echo, not entirely sure what that means.

"No shit, man?" Leo blurts out, pulling his eyes

from the road to stare at Morris.

Morris lands a playful whack on the back of Leo's neck. "Language," he says. "Little ears."

I shake my head, smiling at that. If only Morris knew the things Zoey has heard.

Fucking cunt.

Lying motherfucking bitch.

Asshole traitor of a wife.

All terms of endearment used by my very own husband. He never even bothered to ask Zoey to cover her ears, to leave. She knows she shouldn't say the bad words, but she is not new to hearing them.

I don't bother to share that detail with Morris. He's my bearded, leather-wearing guardian angel. I don't want to give him any reason to regret helping me.

"Sorry, Zoey." Leo twists his head and looks into the back seat. "I used a bad word. Do you have, like, a swear jar or something? Do I have to put in a quarter?"

Zoey's eyes widen, and she looks at Leo adoringly. "Swear jar?" she repeats.

I chuckle. "No, Leo, we never had a swear jar. Zoey knows there are some words grown-ups use that kids should never say. It's okay. Right, baby?"

Zoey nods sleepily, and she stares out the window at the green grass whizzing past the windows.

Now that I'm in the back seat, I don't have to drive, I don't have to concentrate on following the map, so I rest my head against the padded headrest and watch the world roll by. It's been a long time since I could close my eyes against the demands of the day and just let someone else do the heavy lifting.

"So, tell me everything, man. You're in an MC?" Leo, all of a sudden, seems to be fascinated with Morris.

"VP," Morris confirms, nodding.

In the back seat, I'm just inches away from Morris's broad shoulders. He's wearing a light gray T-shirt under his leather vest, and his hair is cropped short on the sides but a little longer on the top. From the back, I can see the freckles dotting the back of his deeply tanned neck and the salt-colored strands of his hair that grow not only in his beard but in the smattering of hair on his muscular arms.

"MC?" I ask lazily, wondering how Morris's shoulders would feel under my hands.

It seems insane that I'm even allowing myself to go there, fantasizing about a man I hardly know, while I'm still technically married to someone else. But Jerry hasn't been the husband of my heart for a very, very long time.

Did we ever have a relationship, I wonder? Or was it always about transactions?

Him paying for my time and company. Me playing the role of the dutiful wife and mother.

Him going full villain the moment the ink dried on our marriage license.

"Motorcycle club," Leo supplies excitedly. "Fuck, man—I mean fudge. Fudge. I have wanted to be in a club since I was a kid!"

"Can you ride?" Morris asks.

"Had my license since I was seventeen," Leo says proudly.

I wonder what the relationship between the two of these guys is. Friends?

Leo seems enamored of Morris, like he's learning things about the man he didn't know. I like getting to know him without having to ask a single question.

Morris nods. "It's a lifestyle, not just a mode of transportation."

"So, wait…" Leo's voice catches. He signals and moves toward the slow lane to exit off the highway. "Are you guys like *Sons of Anarchy* bikers or more like Toys for Tots kind of thing?"

I have no idea what a son of anarchy is, but it sounds dangerous. Unpredictable. Sexy. A lot like Morris. But I do know Toys for Tots.

"We're a little of both," Morris says on a laugh. "We're in the process of changing."

And that, I can most definitely see. Rough and hardened, but not criminal. Protective and abrasive, but sweet, almost teddy-bearish underneath it all. I wonder what a man like Morris is like in bed. I give myself a start, picturing his beard against my body, the delicious friction of his skin against mine. I press my eyes closed to will away the vision.

"Which club, man? What are you guys, like, the Vipers or the Devils?" Leo rattles off several more names that sound more like a list of hazardous animals than the names of anything I'd imagine Morris is a member of.

"We were the Disciples," Morris says. "We have a compound out near where we're headed, but things are gonna be different."

"Why did you buy my brother's place?" Leo asks. "Are you guys expanding? You going to open up another club?"

Morris shakes his head. "Something like that." He turns a little to face me, including me in the conversation. "We just bought a commercial strip mall between Orlando and Daytona," he explains. "Turns out, Leo's brother owned the place before me."

I meet his eyes and mentally add to the list of things this guy is.

Unexpectedly considerate.

Thoughtful.

A business owner.

A biker.

"What do you plan to do with the strip mall?" I ask.

Morris settles back and faces front. "Good question. I was there this morning for the first time, doing some recon on the place. See what's there that's useful, what we need to renovate. We bought it at auction, so no pictures, no inspection ahead of time. Basically bought it sight unseen."

I nod and file that detail away. It kind of fits this man. I can't imagine Jerry doing anything without a team of overpriced blowhard lawyers and years of "due diligence."

Somehow it fits what I already know about Morris —that he'd roll up, buy something, and then just expect it to turn out okay. I wish I had that kind of faith. Maybe it's something I can learn from him.

I rest my head back against the cushion while Leo asks Morris about the club's business, their structure, and how they make money.

Morris seems open to the questions, even the ones that make me wince a little, they're so personal. Almost prying. But I get the sense that Leo's an earnest kid just trying to learn as much as he can. It's like when a fan meets a famous athlete. They want to ask all their questions about how the person does what they do before their few moments with their idol come to an end.

It's sweet, actually.

Morris has his arm on the hard plastic armrest by the window, and I can see he tries to look at me in the passenger side mirror every once in a while.

Our eyes meet, and a warmth floods through my body.

I like this man.

I trust this man.

I haven't felt safe like this, in a car with two virtual strangers, in all the years I've been with Jerry. In as long as I can remember, if I'm being honest. Maybe never.

I smile and close my eyes, listening to the road noises and the deep sound of Morris's voice as the miles slip past.

For a moment, I let myself think about a future. A future without fear. Without that angry voice constantly barking at me, at Zoey, at everything and everyone. Just thinking about Jerry and his voice, his anger, breaks the few moments of peace I have. The stability and calm I let wash over me like a blanket is torn back, and I suddenly feel the chill of the air conditioning on my skin.

I don't know these men.

Morris, Leo. But I do know men.

They start out one way, but then the minute they get what they want, they change. Show their true colors. Zoey's dad did. Jerry after him.

I don't think I need a bearded biker in my life to prove the point. I get it. My daughter and I are on our own. We're gonna need to make our own way.

In a couple days, I'll be in a cheap motel someplace, Zoey will be in a brand-new school, a public school this time, and I'll be serving up blue plate specials, just hoping I make enough in tips to cover after-school care.

I know that's my future.

I know that's what's ahead.

I've been there before, and I'll go back. It's what I have to do to take care of my baby. To take care of myself.

But for a little longer, I'm in the back seat of a big, comfy truck. I have two quiet men who seem to want nothing but to give without exacting a hefty price from me. Jerry doesn't know where I am, and no matter how many times he calls my phone, for a little longer, I can ignore him.

And for a little longer, I can breathe easily, knowing that Morris is inches from my hands.

Without thinking what I'm doing, almost on instinct, I reach a hand past the passenger seat headrest and give Morris's shoulder a quick squeeze. Just a fast, light touch.

Thank you, I think.

It's all I have. No money, no real plans. Just a drive to care for my baby and to keep us both safe. It's something I would not be able to do without help, though. Without Morris.

I close my eyes and pull my hand back. I can tell he's turned his head to look at me, but I won't meet his eyes. I don't want to let myself go there. No need to add fuel to the fire this man sparks in me.

This is one hour of comfort.

One day of friendship.

Then he'll be gone, and I'll be off to whatever passes for a new life.

CHAPTER
SEVEN

MORRIS

BY THE TIME we reach my apartment, both Alice and Zoey are sound asleep. Zoey's in full hibernation, her mouth wide open and her head angled back against the padding of her booster chair.

Alice, if it's even possible, looks more radiant asleep than awake. She's shifted so her head is inclined against the headrest, and she's curled kind of halfway on her side facing Zoey, a protective hand on the booster seat even as she sleeps.

When Leo stops the car, he doesn't immediately kill the engine. "Uh…" he mutters, looking behind him. "They're asleep."

I laugh, quietly, so we don't wake them. The fact that we've stopped and the lack of road noise will wake them soon enough. "Here." I hand him the key to my apartment. "Use the back entrance. The stairs are less narrow than if you go in the front. I'm on the second floor, unit three."

"I'll get the luggage," he says. "What are we gonna do about her car?"

"We'll talk inside," I say and unbuckle my seat belt.

I slip out of the truck and open the rear passenger door by Alice. I admire the extended cab Leo's got going. This truck is surprisingly old, but it's in great shape. If this is any indication of the kind of work the kid does, I have no doubt he'll be able to repair Alice's beater. We'll get her fixed up in no time.

Although, where she'll go when she can leave is another matter.

"Sweetheart?" I don't want to scare her, so I rest a hand on her knee and give her a gentle nudge. "Alice, we're here."

She opens her eyes as if I've fired a shot. She bolts upright and immediately puts her hands in front of her face and ducks down behind them.

I don't have to ask what she's doing.

I've seen it plenty of times before.

She's obviously been awakened one too many times in anger. By someone whose fists were a wake-up call.

The fact that she has to brace herself for even one moment in my presence makes my blood boil. I clench my fists and then realize doing that may stanch my anger, but it only drives the point home to her. I release my hands fast and lean into the back seat.

"It's okay," I assure her, spreading an open hand on the seat. She should be able to see that my hands are nowhere near where they can hurt her. "We're here. You want to wake up the little princess, or should we carry her? I'm on the second floor."

I watch as Alice's expression goes from lost and hiding to gentle realization. She peeks from between her fingers and sees Leo heading into the building, carrying her bags. She looks at me and studies my face for a long minute. She looks away when I meet her eyes directly, but then she looks back.

For a minute, we stare, locked in an exploration so potent, I feel as if she is looking through me.

"Alice?" I echo.

She nods quickly and shakes her head. "I'm sorry," she says, licking her lips. "I dozed off. I was so…" She reaches for her purse and looks at Zoey, fast asleep beside her. "It was nice," she says. "I think that's the most relaxed I've been in…two years."

The boulder in my chest catches fire when she says that.

Two years.

"I'll wake her," Alice says. "She doesn't usually nap anymore. She must have been really worn-out."

"You too," I say, and Alice looks at me again. Through me.

"I was," she agrees. "Am." But with that

admission, the moment between us ends. She turns her attention to Zoey and strokes the little girl's hair. "Zoey," she whispers. She leans close to her daughter's face and gives her a gentle kiss on the cheek.

I watch her wake up her baby, and I am moved by the tenderness between them.

It's been a long time since I've been around kids, and most of the kids I've known have been little wildings, ill-mannered offspring that I had no desire to spend time around kids, let alone talk to. But the raw tenderness between Alice and Zoey makes me think about what I've been missing.

When Jessica talked to me about marriage, about making a life that was more than one night's pleasure at a time, I couldn't picture it. Wouldn't. That domestic life's not for me. I'm not any better suited to diaper duty than I am doing yoga or singing opera.

Fucking, drinking, and riding.

It's what I love, and it's my religion, politics, and lifestyle. My brothers are my family. Family dinners and shit like car seats are for other men.

"Morris?" Alice has inched up to the edge of the bench seat. "She's really out. I may need to carry her. Would you mind grabbing the booster seat?"

She lifts her brows as if to remind me I need to move out of the doorway if I want her to pass by. But I can smell her sugar-cookie sweetness from here, and I'm drunk on it. I flare my nostrils, taking more of it in, all of it I can before I have to move aside and let her pass.

"Yeah," I say, "I got it."

I stand back so she has room to stick a leg out of the back seat, but then she reaches out her hand and holds it. Waiting. For me to take it. Touch her again.

The invitation hits me hard.

She trusts me.

I open my hand, and she grips mine and then jumps down onto the pavement. She smooths the strap of her handbag over her chest, slinging it crossways between her breasts with one hand while she grips my hand in the other. We stand there holding hands for a moment, Alice swaying slightly toward me. Her face is almost pressed against my chest when a small, sleepy voice calls out to us.

"Mama? Where are we?"

Alice drops my hand like it's hot and jerks her head upright. Then she turns and sticks her head back into the truck. "I'm coming around to get you, baby," she says.

She scurries around the front of the truck and opens the driver's side rear door. She has Zoey out of her booster and on the ground before I can catch up.

"You okay? Awake now, Sleeping Beauty? She's a princess, isn't she?" I ask, looking down at the mussed hair and sleep lines on Zoey's face.

Alice looks at me in barely contained surprise, while Zoey seems to have gone from asleep to wide awake in the few seconds it took to get her out of the car.

"Yes, she totally is a princess too," Zoey says. She reaches for my hand and starts walking toward Leo, who is strolling back toward the truck. "Sleeping Beauty's real name is Aurora, so her princess name…"

I turn my head and bug my eyes out at Alice. *Is this okay?* I mouth. This little lady can talk, and she's already down some rabbit hole of princess facts I can't follow. Meanwhile, she's leading me into the apartment building like she's been here a hundred times before.

Alice purses her lips and smiles so big her eyes crinkle shut. She nods and waves us off, and then sticks her head back in the truck, presumably to grab the booster seat.

"Help Alice," I grunt to Leo as he passes me and my miniature chatterbox.

"Will do," Leo says, not bothering to stifle his chuckling.

"Eyes up here," I warn him as he heads toward Alice. "Remember our deal."

I hope he remembers the part of our deal where if he looks at Alice too closely, or even thinks about touching her, I'll turn his nuts into a tailpipe ornament.

"Do you know about Tiana?" Zoey asks. She doesn't wait for a response. "So, she lives in New

Orleans, which is kind of like Florida because it's really hot, but it's not the same."

Zoey continues the explanation, but I've mentally started cataloguing the apartment and what I'll need to make the ladies feel more comfortable.

Groceries, for starters. I doubt I have more than expired mustard in the fridge and, if I'm lucky, at least a couple beers and some bottled water.

I've got one bedroom and one bath, but I'm sure Alice can share with Zoey, or she can give Zoey the bed and she can sleep on the couch. It's an L-shaped sectional that I can say from experience is sleep-worthy, given the many, many times I've passed out there, too drunk to even make it into bed.

As Zoey and I take the back steps, my education on princesses' real names continuing, my phone rings.

"Goddamn, Tiny." It slips out before I can stop myself. "Sorry, princess. Bad word."

Zoey seems unfazed as she climbs with me up the stairs. I let her into the apartment, releasing her hand long enough to pick up the call.

"Tiny, for—" I lower my voice to a whisper so I can drop the bomb"—fuck's sake! What?"

"Morris," Tiny says, sounding as put out with me as I am with him. "Where you been, man? I been trying to reach you all day!"

"I've had some complications with the property," I say. I point to the couch and watch as Zoey plunks down on the edge of a cushion. She sits primly and folds her hands, waiting for me. Probably waiting for me to finish my call so she can pick up the conversation where we left off. Which, if I'm not mistaken, was someplace in the middle of the plot of *Brave*. I've lost count of the princesses at this point.

"I've had fucking complications here too. That's why I've been calling." Tiny sounds off. Stressed.

"What is it? Club trouble?" I'd really love to deal with one goddamn thing at a time, but that's not the nature of the brotherhood. This man is more my family than my family—what's left of it—is.

"Nah, it's more…personal."

"All right. Can it wait? I'm in the middle of—"

"Yeah, I guess. But I need a favor. You using your apartment right now?"

That stops me in my tracks. "As a matter of fact, I am. Why? You need it?"

Tiny is one of the brothers who doesn't have any place to hang his hat other than the compound. Tiny loves the compound and rarely talks about life outside the club. I think the guy was married once, or had an old lady long ago. But something like this, needing my place… This is a first.

"Maybe," he says.

Fuck.

"All right. I'm here at my apartment now, and I've got company. I'll get back to you as soon as I can. This can wait?"

"Yeah, yeah…" Tiny sounds far away, but right

now, I've got a little girl kicking her shoes and fidgeting on my couch. She looks like she's about to burst.

"Man, I gotta go. I'll get back to you." I end the call and walk over to Zoey just as Alice and Leo are coming up the stairs.

"You okay?" I ask the kid. "You need something?"

She looks at her mom and nods.

"What is it, honey?" Alice drops the booster chair on the floor by the door.

"I have to use the bathroom," Zoey says loudly.

Leo starts to grin, and Alice takes her daughter by the hand.

I breathe a huge sigh of relief. That, I can do.

"One sec," I say, holding up a finger. I wanna make sure there's nothing in there that would traumatize a kid or Alice. I'm not here much, but it wouldn't surprise me to find a used condom floating in the toilet…or worse.

I flip on the light and inspect the toilet for offensive material. Finding none, I scan the sink for soap— check. And the hand towel looks as clean as the ones in the closet. One last look to make sure there's toilet paper, and I think we're good to go. But then it hits me.

"Alice?" I say, sticking my head into the hallway.

She walks through the small apartment, hand in hand with Zoey.

"Does she need like one of those seats for the

shitter—I mean, the toilet? Don't kids need like potty boosters?"

Alice covers her mouth with a hand and giggles, while Zoey charges past me to the toilet.

"I haven't needed one of those since I was four!" she declares. She shuts the door behind herself and calls, "Thanks!"

Alice pinches her eyebrows between two fingers and lets out a full-blown laugh. "Potty boosters... You're not around kids much, are you?"

I shake my head. "Today might be a lifetime record."

"Really?" she asks. "No little Morris babies running around out there? No wife?" She hesitates on that last question like she is embarrassed to ask it.

I take that opportunity to lean close to her. Her sunshine hair is spilling over her shoulders, and she's pushed the sunglasses up onto her head so I can look right into those caramel-brown eyes.

"Now, why the sudden interest in my personal life?" I ask. I'm careful not to cage my beautiful bird in, but oh fuck, how I want to.

I want to pin her against the wall of my hallway and bury my face in her hair. Taste her neck, bite down on the sinews of her lean shoulders. Soon, maybe. But not now. Not yet.

She meets my eyes and, this time, doesn't look away. "Who says it's sudden?" she teases, her voice thick. "I've been curious about you since the hot dog stand."

I nod and play along.

"You seemed, let's just say, guarded. Not exactly what I would call interested," I say, but I soften my words by picking up a bit of that sunshine hair. I rub the strands between my fingers. Fuck, she feels as soft as she looks.

Alice swallows, and I hear her breaths, in and out. Deep and shaky. But not with fear. Her pupils dilate, and she lifts her chin. A brazen move for my shaky little sparrow.

"Mom?" The door suddenly flies open, and Zoey is standing there with her hands on her hips.

"Yeah, Zo, what is it?"

"Can you fix my hair? It got all messy when I fell asleep." Zoey's scowling as if she just noticed she has a bad case of car-ride bed head.

"Yeah, of course." Alice draws her lower lip into her mouth.

I watch her bite it, and slowly, she releases the swollen skin from between her teeth.

She steps away from my hold and starts chattering with Zoey about quickly redoing her braid.

I stand in the hallway a moment, watching them and listening. Zoey's voice is light and sweet, and Alice is reassuring and calm as she pulls off the princess baseball cap and uses her fingers to smooth out Zoey's braid. She quickly works the hair into this new complicated thing and then replaces the hat.

"Love it?" Alice asks, lifting Zoey up so she can inspect the entire hairdo in the mirror.

"Love it," Zoey says. "Now can we eat?"

Alice meets my eyes and shrugs.

"I could do with some grub," Leo calls from the living room.

I shake my head and grin. "I guess that means we're eating."

CHAPTER EIGHT

ALICE

WE ORDER sandwiches from a place up the street, and Leo offers to walk over to pick them up.

Morris nods and gives Leo some cash.

"Would you mind grabbing juice or water for Zoey?" I ask.

"'Course not," he says. He gives Zoey a smile. "You wanna walk over with me? You can pick out your own drink."

My stomach clenches at that. This kid is a stranger to me, and while I appreciate that his intentions are probably pure...the key word there is probably.

Before I can put together some kind of polite excuse, Morris claps Leo on the shoulder.

"You don't have kids or a girlfriend, do ya, kid?" He doesn't say it in a shitty way. If I'm not mistaken, Morris almost sounds fond of Leo.

Leo's face flames red, and he shakes his head and shrugs. "Why? What'd I say?"

Morris gives me a wink and pulls Leo a little closer. "My guests here have had a lot of excitement with strangers this morning, and even though you and I know we're the good guys—" Morris's voice holds a subtle note of warning, making it clear he is telling Leo he'd damn well better be one of the good ones "—I think Zoey probably would rather stay close to her mom for a while."

Leo looks at me and then Morris, as if it finally is hitting him that maybe it would be weird that he offered to take my six-year-old child out into the world alone.

I love Leo a little bit in that moment. The fact that he is part of a world where a young man offering to take a little girl he doesn't know to pick up lunch isn't scary, isn't potentially dangerous.

I envy him that innocence. I can't remember a time when I didn't think through the risks of any situation eight thousand different ways before diving in. I only hope I can create a bubble for Zoey where she can move freely through her world with fears and dangers being much easier to spot. Where the fear and danger don't come from within her own home. From the man who is supposed to love and protect her.

Eventually.

I nod at Morris, and Leo mumbles an apology.

"I didn't think… I didn't mean…"

"No, no," I reassure him. "It's okay. Thanks, Leo."

Zoey is standing by quietly, listening intently to the adults, and I don't want to draw any more attention to the conversation we've been having.

"Come on, sweetheart," I say. "Morris, would you mind if we kick off our shoes and sit down for a bit?"

"Sit down for a bit? Nah, nah, nah. We're going to get you settled and comfortable." Morris grabs the remote control to the TV and gives it a look. "Now, have a seat anywhere you like, little lady."

Zoey peers down at her stained dress. "But what about the juice?"

Morris stares at me in confusion. "Is it dry?"

Zoey nods, but doesn't move otherwise.

"Doesn't matter. I'm sure the couch has had worse on it." He looks at me when he says those words and grimaces, knowing what he said wasn't meant for young ears or even mine.

I throw Zoey a look, trying not to laugh at Morris, and she nods, then walks to the front door and slips off her shoes. She pads back to the long sectional couch and sits down on the edge, smoothing her dress over the cushions.

Morris hasn't made much progress with the TV. "Fu—fudge," he says. "It's been a while since I watched any TV here. I don't stay here all that often, and when I do… Well, I have all the streaming services, if you're allowed to watch... I'll figure this out."

Zoey's eyes are wide as she watches Morris try to turn the TV on and then off again.

None of the buttons seem to respond, no matter in what order he presses them. The seconds stretch into minutes as Morris tries and tries to get the remote to work.

Her little face is perfectly still and patient.

"I'll be..." Morris mutters. He throws me a look. "I'm not much for this stuff. TV. Technology."

"Mama," Zoey says so quietly I almost can't hear her.

"Yeah, baby?" I walk over to the couch and stroke her hair.

Zoey motions for me to move closer. I bring my ear near her face so she can whisper. "Is he mad?" she asks. "I don't have to watch TV."

I look at Morris to see if he's heard Zoey's question. I can immediately tell he has.

His expression transforms before my eyes from sweet confusion to irritation. It's a metamorphosis I know all too well. And goddamn, it's not something I'm going to let happen again. Whether he's saved my ass today or not, he has a temper, and I'm not going to stay here and let this happen to us. Not again. They always start out so goddamn charming.

I'm shocked at the rush of disappointment that

washes over me. For a minute—just a minute—I really let myself believe Morris could be different. That some other kind of man exists. Not just Jerrys or versions of Jerry with bigger arms and bikes.

"Mad?" Morris barks, his voice loud after Zoey's whisper. "I'm mad that I can't seem to operate a simple remote control. I'm smarter than I seem right now," he says, shaking his head. He holds the remote out to us. "Any chance Princess Zoey can run this thing? Kids always seem to know how to do everything better than adults."

Zoey looks at me with a question in her eyes, but I have to look away.

He's not mad. Not at her, anyway. Not at the blameless reality of life where things just happen. He's not mad.

We both expected it, and now that I know he's not angry at my daughter, that he's not going to blow up and make her feel guilty for just being there, I don't know what to say or what to do.

"I can do it," she tells him softly, her eyes looking down at her socks.

"Well, sure you can, darlin'. Let's just make sure it's all right with your mama." Morris holds the remote like it is made of glass and he is afraid he's going to break it. He flips it over and presses the button, and then gives it a shake. "I think the battery might be dead…" he mutters. "I mean, I really thought…"

I lift my head to look at him, hoping that every emotion running through my body in that moment isn't written plain on my face.

Surprise. Shock. Gratitude. Relief.

"Zoey means she can operate the remote," I explain.

Morris quirks a brow at me but passes the remote to my daughter. "Have at it, little lady," he says.

Zoey nods and presses her lips together to bite back her excitement.

And even that, my daughter's joy that she is going to be allowed to try to operate the remote, guts me. She is used to keeping quiet in the car whenever we were with Jerry. He preferred that she play in her room alone or go to friends' houses to keep play dates away from his home.

Zoey is courteous and attentive and has great manners, far beyond her six years. She knows her place, well-trained through two years of yelling, anger, and acting out. Not by her. She is the child, but Jerry is the one who threw tantrums. Dangerous, terrible tantrums.

Within a matter of seconds, Zoey has the television set on, and she's launched the app for a streaming service on the screen.

"It needs your password," she says sweetly. "You really haven't watched TV in a long time!" She seems to be able to roll with this new energy much more easily than I am. She gives Morris a delighted smile. "I can type it in if you know what it is."

Morris coughs lightly into his hand. "Oh, shiiii… shucks. I don't think I can even remember my password." He looks at me with a pained expression on his face.

"She's got this," I reassure him.

"Okay," Zoey says, taking charge. She stands from the couch and walks up to Morris. "Do you have an e-mail address? I can help you reset your password, but you'll need to get into your e-mail."

I nod at Morris, urging him to trust my daughter. He pulls his phone from his pocket and starts opening apps. I need a minute to process what I'm seeing. What's changing right before my eyes.

Zoey, in a matter of minutes, went from that same scared little thing that I saw to her bright, happy self. The self I saw whenever I was alone with my daughter. The self I adored and nurtured and would do anything for. The self I wasn't going to allow to be hidden or harmed anymore.

And while we both have a long way to go, watching Morris and Zoey work on resetting the password together brings me a feeling I haven't had in a long time—peace.

But of course, I can't let the moment last. While I know Zoey is safe and working her way into being able to watch TV, our problems won't be quite so easily solved.

I grab my phone and check my missed calls.

Four.

I have four missed calls from Jerry.

Factoring in the time difference, Jerry shouldn't be expecting a check-in call from me to confirm that we landed for at least another three hours.

My heart races. He's left three messages, but for some reason, he didn't leave a message after the fourth call. Morris and Zoey are still hunched over his phone, resetting his password.

"Okay, now pick something easy to remember and easy to spell, Morris." Zoey is giving out sage advice. "You don't want to forget it or have to type it in a hundred times because you keep spelling it wrong."

"Okay," Morris says, taking this whole task very seriously. "What do you think? MyTV?" He curls his lips into a silly grin, and the way the trimmed beard spreads over a dimple in his cheek gives me an unfamiliar tingle inside. He's so goddamn...cute.

Zoey starts to giggle, a high-pitched sound. "That's a terrible password! You want to pick something that nobody can easily guess. How about Tiana?"

"Okay." Morris tries punching that into his phone but then stops. "How are we spelling that? Two n's or just one?"

Zoey spells it out letter for letter and watches as Morris dutifully punches in the keys on his phone.

"Nope." He shrugs at her. "No can do Tiana. It's

telling me here I need numbers and something. Look at this."

My heart nearly shatters as I watch this enormous, tattooed biker try to reset his password on his phone with my daughter's help. He hands her his phone, and I shake my head, wondering if Morris even knows that Tiana is a Disney princess. I'm starting to suspect that even if he does know, he doesn't much care.

"We did it!" Zoey squeals, interrupting my thoughts.

Morris looks as pleased as she does, his bright eyes twinkling as he adjusts the sound down on the set, which had come to life at what seemed like full volume. "Well done, kiddo!" He holds his hand up to high-five Zoey, and to my absolute shock, she smashes her hand against his.

She plops down on the couch like she owns the place, all the ladylike skirt-smoothing and formalities of before gone. "Are you gonna watch with me?" she asks politely. "You can pick now that we have the TV on."

Morris laughs so loudly and so sincerely, I feel another ounce of tension evaporate from my shoulders.

"You pick, princess. This is all you." Morris covers half of his mouth with his hand and stage-whispers, "But I might need you to write down those instructions for me later."

Zoey giggles and tucks her feet under her. She points the remote at the TV, and before I even say a word, she calls out, "Don't worry, Mommy. I'm creating a kids channel right now."

I nod at her. "Good job, honey."

Morris looks confused.

"Some of the trailers and even the preview thumbnails can be pretty scary for kids. Most sites allow you to create a kids channel with your service. So kids can browse the choices without seeing anything too adult."

"Huh? No shit?" Morris says, looking pleasantly surprised. "I mean, no… Ah, forget it." He scrubs a hand across the back of his neck. "Old dog here. It's gonna be a while before I can learn some new tricks."

I study his face for clues. Just a few minutes ago, I'd thought I was about to see the mask peel away. The gremlin, the monster, the demon behind the dimpled smile and salt-and-pepper beard baring his teeth. But Morris is looking at me sweetly, studying me as I study him.

I notice him looking at my phone.

"Speaking of adult time," he says, his voice low, a hint of flirtation in his tone.

Morris's voice is so…sexy. It's like friction and movement and light bouncing between his lips. I can imagine what it would feel like to lie against his chest and hear that gritty rasp against my ears.

"Alice?" he says softly, and it's as if he can read my thoughts. He moves closer to me, but not close enough to touch me. Just close enough that if I wanted to, I could lean forward. Rest my head against that chest again, close my eyes, and let everything I'm running from fade away for a few minutes. Escape. Peace. Release. Just thinking about him like this has my nipples tightening beneath my tank top, my core sparking to life.

My face heats, and I feel like an asshole.

I can't think of this man like he's…a man. I can't let myself be distracted by dimples and smiles or the sensual way the graying stubble trails down his neck.

I have a husband to leave and a daughter to provide for. And those two things are all there's room for. Nothing else. No one else. I have to stop the damsel-in-distress act. I'm not a Disney princess. There is no such thing as Prince Charming.

Morris rode into my life on a motorcycle, not a white horse. And as soon as we figure out our next move, this chapter will end, and I'll be on to a totally different story. One that leaves this sweet, sexy biker in the rearview mirror.

"Yeah? Yes?" I snap my face to his, willing away the mess my thoughts have become. Jerry. Morris. Zoey. Morris. Morris.

I'm on this endless loop of watching and worrying, and suddenly, I'm fucking tired.

But whatever Morris has to say to me will have to wait. There's a light knock at the door, and then Leo toes the door open and holds up two big white paper bags. He looks proud of himself.

"Food is here!" he calls.

CHAPTER NINE

MORRIS

WHILE ALICE LAYS out the sandwiches and gets Zoey set up to eat, Leo and I stand together in my small kitchen, trying to figure out what to do about Alice's car.

"You want me to haul it back to the yard?" Leo asks. "You give me three to four days and the cash I need to buy whatever parts I don't have, and she'll be good to go."

"How much you thinking?" I ask. "Didn't you strip the shop of everything that wasn't nailed down?"

I'm giving him a hard time, but it's also a real question. I can imagine a repair like that won't be cheap. And I think three days is optimistic, especially for a kid working alone.

"Well, that depends," Leo says. He meets my eyes and explains that the power's been off, so he can't technically put the car up in a bay for a full diagnostic. "You get the power back on, I'll know much faster what the car needs. And"—he looks embarrassed as he admits it—"if I have the parts back at my house, I won't have to buy 'em."

"You need a job? You'll do the work? Can I trust you?" I motion to the bruise forming on his face. "A couple hours ago, you and me… We weren't on such friendly terms."

Leo rubs the spot on his face and shrugs. "I won't hold a grudge if you won't."

I consider the kid for a minute. I'm not long on trust, but unless I want to fork over more cash to a stranger and spend more time getting Alice's car towed, Leo working off his debt to me seems to make good sense.

I watch Leo's face as I explain the deal.

"Here's how this is gonna go. I'll get the power back on at your brother's old shop. You fix Alice's car with what parts you have. Anything you need, and I mean anything, you come to me. I'll buy it and bring it to you. No cash, no funny business. You donate the labor, and I'll buy the parts to get your granddaddy's car working so you can drive it off my lot."

I calculate in my head how much we're probably talking. It's a fair deal for the kid, actually. More than fair. But I ask him to be sure, more of a statement than a question.

"Fair?" I say.

"I don't know." Leo shakes his head. "That truck

could need two, three grand in parts, Morris. I don't think it's gonna cost that much in time and inventory to get Alice's car running. I'm gonna owe you. And I don't know how I'll be able to pay you back that kind of cash."

I'm real proud of the boy in this moment. He is laying it to me straight. Not trying to manipulate or abuse the situation. A lesser man would have known he was getting the better end of the deal and kept his trap shut. But Leo's clearly not a lesser man.

"You're working off your debt to me," I explain. "And, in turn, you're gonna help me get that yellow hunk of junk off my property. Sounds like a real fair deal to me. I don't think I need numbers to jive this. I'm good, so…we good?"

I give a half smirk to let him know I'm not really insulting his granddaddy's truck.

"Now, come on," I say. "We got sandwiches waiting."

Leo stares at me for a moment, like he's not sure whether to hug me or slug me. I clap him on the shoulder and open the refrigerator on instinct, hoping for some cold beer to wash down lunch. I moan at what I see. I'm gonna need to do some shopping.

It takes some convincing before Alice lets Leo haul her car away. She's clinging to that dead hunk of junk like it's her last lifeline to freedom.

And it probably is, but at this point, it's not going to get her anywhere. This little bird's broken a wing, and without it, she ain't flying.

Before Leo leaves, I give the kid explicit instructions to move my bike into the building to secure it overnight. He really wanted the keys, offered at least six different times to ride it back here to me, but there was no way I was letting any man's ass on my ride.

I trusted he could lock it in the repair bay, since it turned out Leo had a master set of keys for every door in the strip mall anyway. We exchanged numbers, and I told him I'd be by the shop tomorrow to get my bike. I figured I'd have Tiny or one of the Disciples drive me over.

For a couple bucks in gas, shit, I could get Midge to drive me. Although, knowing Midge, she'll wanna throw in a BJ as part of the deal. She works over at the compound doing anything and anyone that needs doing.

Although I wouldn't consider letting Midge near my dick on a good day, with Alice nearby, I won't even entertain the idea for fun.

I can't explain the way I react to her.

Alice is beautiful, sure. Her body is firm and yet soft, her ass plush and enticing in a way that makes me want to bend her over any available surface and taste her skin with my teeth.

But there's something else there. Something more.

The ease I feel with her and Zoey isn't something I'm used to. Hell, it's not something I ever thought possible.

I've never been that guy.

Never wanted to be tied down to people.

I love coming home to my room.

My shit.

The satisfying crack of the tab on a beer as I have a drink after a long ride. There's no room at the compound for a kid, for family. And I have no desire to ever leave the club.

I have everything I've ever wanted. Freedom. All the fun I can stand. And a place to call home—my room at the compound.

But having Alice and Zoey here, I realize this place could be more than a crash pad.

It could be someone's home.

Alice is clearing away the mess from our meal, opening and closing the cabinets, looking for the trash bin and cleaning supplies. She is making herself at home, busying herself and stealing little looks at me.

I just watch her. I lean back in my chair and cross my arms. Zoey is finishing the last bite of her chips. Alice looks flustered as she sweeps the crumbs from in front of Leo's place.

"Mama," Zoey asks quietly. "May I be excused?"

Alice faces her daughter, but she looks tired. Too tired. "Yeah, baby, of course. You gonna finish that movie?"

Zoey nods and leaps excitedly from the chair.

"Zoey?" Alice stops her with a gentle tone. A reminder. "Morris treated us today. Did you forget to say thank you?"

Zoey spins on her little blue socks and races up to me. "Thank you so much for that sandwich, Morris," she says. "It was really good!" She holds her hand up for a high five, and I lightly lift my palm to meet hers.

"My pleasure, princess," I say. "Now, go have some fun."

Alice is watching me with a look on her face I can't read. She doesn't look angry or unhappy, but more…uncertain.

"So," I say after Zoey is settled on the couch. "Leo's going to take care of your car."

"Morris…" Alice sighs. "I can't afford to get it fixed. I can't…"

I shake my head and motion for her to sit. "I didn't say anything about paying for it, sweetheart."

Alice's face falls even more. She drops down into the chair beside me, hunches her shoulders over, and rests her face in her hands. "I had a plan…" she explains. "I prepared for every possibility. Months," she says, sounding more and more defeated. "And the one thing I didn't expect is the one thing that's going to ruin everything." She trails off into silence and closes her eyes. "I can never repay you for what you've already done. I don't think I can ever repay Leo and you for what you're about to do."

"Baby," I say, reaching a hand across the table. I scoot my chair a little closer to hers. Our knees brush under my kitchen table and I notice she doesn't move away, but she flinches a little, as if surprised at first, and then she relaxes. The warmth of her thigh suddenly lines up against mine, and I feel her heat in my cock. "What's this plan? It's time you level with me."

Alice draws a shaky breath and shakes her head. "I don't want to involve you any more than I already have. I can't—"

"Alice." I clap my hand over her knee under the table. I give her a gentle squeeze and leave my hand there. If she looks uncomfortable, I'll take it away, but right now, I need her focused on me. On telling me everything I need to know. "Who are you running from?" I ask. "Husband, boyfriend? Baby daddy?"

Alice shakes her head and clamps her mouth shut.

"Alice."

I look behind us into the living room, making sure that Zoey's watching TV. The little princess is totally preoccupied by a cartoon princess kicking some ass against a squad of bad guys with a dagger. Is this what kids watch these days?

"Alice," I repeat, bringing my attention back to

the beauty beside me. But this time, I lift her chin with my hand.

If she's going to ignore me, she's going to have to do it looking me dead in the eye.

I raise her chin, and she flicks her eyes to meet mine. But once I have her skin under my fingers, I can't help myself. Her sugary scent draws me closer, and I stroke the ridge of her chin softly with my thumb. My dick reacts to that light touch, and I have to release her before I go full animal on her.

Jesus, what this woman does to me.

I want to sucker-punch the fucker who put those shadows under her caramel eyes. The light purple bags make her look tired and lonely. Like she's been running a long, long time.

If I could pull her close and shred the assholes in her world like that TV princess, I'd do it with my bare hands. No dagger required. But first, I need to know what the fuck she's dealing with.

"My husband," she admits. "He's…an asshole," she supplies.

I drop my hand from her skin, which draws both of us out of the sensual haze.

"Zoey's dad?" I ask.

The answer to that one simple question will make everything either a hell of a lot harder or a hell of a lot simpler.

She shakes her head. "No. I think that's why all this is so fucking triggering," she explains. "When I met Jerry, I was working as a waitress, a single mom with a four-year-old. He owned the car dealership across the street, and for months, he worked me over. Coming in, waiting to sit at one of my tables, leaving really big tips."

Alice sighs, her shoulders sagging even lower. She plays with the ends of her hair and avoids my eyes like she's embarrassed or ashamed.

"In my eyes, sweetheart." I lift her chin again. I can't stand to see the fear worrying her face.

"I didn't want to date him. I really didn't." She meets my eyes and laughs, a frustrated, ironic laugh. "He had that slightly slimy vibe, you know?"

She sighs.

"But he was charming too, and he was really persistent. Begged me to just let him take me to dinner. And eventually, I caved. One dinner led to two, and within three months, he gave me a huge ring."

She holds up her unadorned left hand. She chuckles a wry laugh. "I sold the ring to buy that fucking car," she laughed. "I should have known."

"Jesus." I can't help myself. "You traded in an engagement ring for a whole goddamned car?"

She sighs. "Jerry was all sparkle, no substance. Just like our marriage. Just like that car. I got taken for a ride yet again."

"And let me guess, the blush was off the rose by

what, the end of the honeymoon?" I ask. "When did the mask come off?"

"Well, we didn't go on a honeymoon," Alice says. "I had Zoey to think about. He made me quit the job as soon as he proposed. He didn't like how it would look to his clients and business partners if his wife worked in a greasy diner. I'm qualified to do other things," Alice says, her voice suddenly small. "I didn't finish college, but I have an associate's in business. I just… Well, that's another failure."

"You're not a failure," I snap, a little more harshly than I planned.

She looks surprised by the tone of my voice, but she continues. "Oh, wait," she says, half bitter, half ironic. "I am. My college boyfriend left me when I got pregnant. That's how I ended up waitressing with a four-year-old. He ended up with a scholarship from a university out west. He said a kid and no degree weren't in the cards for him. He knew I was pregnant, but he just transferred. And since he was out of state and I was broke, pregnant, and twenty-two, I just didn't have the money to pursue him. He's never even met Zoey."

"And this Jerry character? He married you but didn't adopt Zoey?"

I can't imagine what kind of piece of shit gives his wife a sparkler worth as much as a car but who doesn't adopt the child he is responsible for helping to raise.

"That was never on the table," she says simply. "I mean, it literally never came up. I think in the back of Jerry's mind, Zoey would always be just mine, my problem, my responsibility. In fact, the older she got, the worse things became between us. When she was four and was in day care all day while I worked and while we dated, I think he was able to pretend I didn't really have a kid. But once we moved in to his house…"

I clench my fists, bracing for what comes next. "Did he—"

The color must be flooding my face because suddenly, I feel a soft hand on my bicep.

"No, Morris. Not Zoey. He never laid a hand on her." Alice's voice is so, so small. I can't comprehend what it feels like to have a child, to be responsible for a beautiful little life like Zoey's, and to be beholden to anyone to provide for her.

"I would hunt him down and kill him right on that goddamn showroom floor if he did." I can picture it now, the image of this fuckwad's jaw when my fist hits it freeing a little bit of the rage building up in my chest. "You sure?" I press. "You'd tell me."

She blinks fast and smiles. "I would tell you. I trust you," she says.

And somehow, it feels like an invitation. One that I know I won't refuse.

But then as quick as the light came on, it goes out.

"But there are so many ways to hurt a woman," she adds quietly.

The heat explodes in my chest again as I throttle back the rage her words bring. I know guys like this. Shit, had my circumstances been different, I might have been a guy like that. But my mother died of breast cancer when I was young, and my old man was a miserable prick.

I spent my teenage years taking care of things no kid should ever have to care for. It's not something I linger on, but it occurs to me now that maybe that's why I never wanted to have a family of my own.

"He's not going to hurt you ever again," I say quietly under my breath.

"Morris," she says, shaking her head. "You don't know what he's capable of."

"If you think that, darlin', then you don't know what I'm capable of."

CHAPTER
TEN
ALICE

AFTER OUR TALK, Morris makes a couple phone calls, and I take a few minutes to check my messages.

As I punch in the code to my voice mail, I start regretting that I ate at all. The sandwich sits like a rock in my belly, and I have to breathe in through my nose and slowly out through my mouth to ease the waves of nausea rolling through my body.

You can do this, I remind myself. *He can't find me. He can't hurt me.*

And that's the truth, isn't it?

I can breathe easy.

I'm safe.

But the pep talk falls flat even as I give it to myself. I snuggle up on the couch next to Zoey, who immediately curls against me and settles in. I grip my phone in a clammy hand, and I follow Morris with my gaze.

He's leaning against the kitchen counter, his legs crossed at the ankle. His jeans are well broken-in, the thin patches over his knees just barely breaking through to his skin. The denim fits his thighs like the jeans were made for his body, and I follow the lines of his muscular form until I reach his face. He's holding his phone with one hand and is talking in a low voice, but the deep rumble reaches me all the way across the apartment.

I can't explain what it is about this man, but his presence calms me. He's a solid mountain of mass. Just being in the same room with him makes me *feel* so different. The way he walks, holds his body, even the way he stands still, completely focused on the phone call he's on… He's so different from the frantic, erratic way Jerry is constantly moving, shifting, yelling, doing.

Morris's body is huge, his arms nearly as wide around as my thigh. The salt-and-pepper beard is trimmed close to his face, so I can make out the contours of his chin and lips. He has a beautiful mouth. His lips are average, not too full and not thin, but it's his smile, that full grin, his square white teeth that soften the look of a man who otherwise could be even more imposing than Jerry.

The lightness in him comes out when he smiles. As he talks now, he's scowling, but I can remember some of the smiles he's gifted me with so far. At the gas station. On the drive here. Talking to Zoey.

How such a rough giant can make me feel more at peace than I've felt in years is…a mystery. But I say a silent prayer of thanks to the angels who led him to help me. I know I'm strong. It took heart and commitment and guts to plan this escape. And I made it. I made it out. I'm out from under Jerry's control, and I never, ever have to go back. I just have to get through the next few hours. Jerry finding out that I didn't go to my sister's. His rage when he realizes it's over. But I'm so close. I'm like a bird trapped in a cage. I finally pried open the door and can see the way out. I just need to stay out of sight of the cat until I find a new perch.

Morris catches me looking at him and waggles his brows once. He sees me watching him. And he's eyeing me too. That moment of playfulness feels almost normal. Almost real.

Like the asshole whose voice I'm used to hearing or the scary messages I'm dreading listening to are nothing more than an annoyance from my past. Something to get done and get through so I can get back to the good stuff that I have now. Jerry is trash be put out and taken away forever.

Zoey adjusts her head on the back of the couch, so I close my eyes and draw in one more breath. I half wish I could stand near Morris while I do this. Somehow, his closeness would make this feel easier.

But at the same time, I don't want anything having to do with Jerry anywhere near Morris. I want to get through this and put Jerry Cruz in my rearview mirror as fast as humanly possible.

I punch in the voice mail password and listen to the first message.

Babe.

Jerry's voice is clipped in the first message he left this morning. Based on the time stamp, he called just about an hour after my flight should have taken off.

Just wanted to wish you a safe flight and a good trip.

His voice sounds strained, tight. The tone doesn't match the words he's saying. Then he says:

Make sure you call me the second you land. I wanna hear from you before you deplane. Do you understand? Call me the minute you land.

I understand him, all right. This isn't bad, but it's not good either. He wants to know my first thought when we land is of him. My first call is to him. I almost delete the message on instinct, but then I decide to wait. I don't know what's coming, and it can't hurt to delete them all at once. Or hold on to them…if I need to.

I press play and listen to the second message, which came in not long after the first.

Alice… Zoey's iPad was turned off this morning before you even boarded the plane. Maybe you dropped it. Forgot to charge it. You can be a real shithead when it comes to the small details. I wouldn't put anything past you. I'm going to drive over to the airport lot and see if the iPad is there. You better hope I don't find it, Alice. You better hope I don't find anything I'm not expecting.

My hands start to shake before the message even ends. He knows Zoey's iPad is turned off. *Before* we were supposed to board the plane. Why would he check? He'd have no reason to check the location tracker on my daughter's iPad while he expected us to be at the airport. Why did he?

I swallow hard and notice Morris lift his face to me. He's studying me, so I force a tight smile and try to lean back against the cushions.

I need to listen to the last message. There are a few missed calls, but for some reason, Jerry only left three messages. Two down, one to go.

I curl my toes and swallow against the panic fluttering in my throat like the wings of a hummingbird, beating fast and making my chest nearly vibrate with anticipation.

Alice. Alice. Alice. You filthy fucking bitch. So, you're not in Denver after all. I should have known. I should have expected as much. You don't give a shit about your cunt sister and spring break. But don't worry, baby. I'm coming to bring you home. I'll see you tonight. I'm coming to get you.

My mouth falls open, and as I drop my phone, I let a tiny yelp slip through my lips. He knows.

He knows.
He knows.
He knows.

My thoughts race, and my palms are suddenly clammy. The room spins slightly, but I can't be sure if the movement is in my head or if it's the sudden appearance of Morris in front of me, blocking my view and blurring my vision. I can hardly focus on him.

I'm falling down a hole, a deep, dark pit where Jerry waits for me. I can feel his presence for the first time since I left. Like an invisible chain, he's got me shackled to him emotionally, mentally. He knows I didn't go to Denver.

He knows I'm not with my sister... My sister. I need to call her.

"*Alice!*" Morris's voice snaps me out of the whirlwind of racing thoughts.

I must look pale and terrified because Morris's eyes are wide like he's afraid I'm going to faint. I know I will if I stand too fast, but at this point, oblivion would be better than the anguish I'm feeling.

I was supposed to have hours of lead time.

I was supposed to get away before Jerry even knew I was gone.

I was supposed to...

Suddenly, a large hand takes mine, and Morris tugs me from the couch. "Excuse us a minute, little lady," he says to Zoey.

I can't find words or even my footing. All I see is Jerry's face, close to mine. I swear I can feel his breath on my neck, the pressure of his palm on the back of my head as he holds me against the mattress. It's his favorite way to control me. His favorite way to exact my compliance.

I blink against the memory, feeling the down comforter stifling the flow of air to my mouth and nose. I feel the strength in his hold, as if my body can feel the way he's fighting for control over how much he will hurt me. He likes hurting me. It's not sudden or violent, but gradual and harsh. I can almost hear him thinking about how much air he's going to steal from my lungs before he lies on top of me and whispers in my ear.

"Baby, come on back to me. Alice, baby." I hear the voice and blink, trying to bring Morris's face into focus.

As I look around the room, I realize I am in a bedroom, sitting on a bed with soft, fluffy blankets folded at the bottom. A hand-sewn quilt hangs on the wall behind the bed, an odd wall-covering in a room otherwise fairly barren. We must be in Morris's bedroom. The door is open and I can still hear the TV, so I know Zoey isn't far. But I have no memory of walking in here.

I swallow again and will my heart to slow, to steady its frantic beats. I nod my head and rock slightly back and forth, gripping the blankets in my fists. "He knows," I whisper. "He knows I ran. He's coming for me."

Morris doesn't say a word. He grabs my hand and

pulls me to standing. Before him, I'm weak. Fragile. Powerless. Prey.

Before I can think twice about it, I practically fall against Morris's chest. This space is becoming familiar, welcome. The moment my body touches his, I'm wrapped in his arms, and he holds me close.

"Not gonna happen, baby," he says. He shushes against my hair. "I got you. You're safe. Zoey is safe. I got you."

I shake my head against the mass of this man. "You don't… I can't…" It's impossible to put into words. How stupid I feel.

How did I think I could leave Jerry?

How did I think he'd just let me get away?

I realize in a rush I have to call my sister.

I have to warn her.

He could do anything.

He is capable of…

"Alice."

As my name rumbles through Morris's chest, I lean back and meet his gaze. Tears burn my eyes, and I blink hard. I know what comes after this. The stillness. The shutting down. It is a predictable pattern. First, the fear. Then, I freeze.

But this time, the predictable cold doesn't flood my veins. Instead, fire scorches my skin as Morris grips my chin in his hand.

"Alice, baby," he says. "Come here."

I follow the movement of his hand on my chin.

It's so easy. My body is functioning on autopilot, letting Morris lead me wherever he wants to go. In my weakened state, he could probably do anything to me, and I'd be powerless to fight. Just like I am with Jerry.

But instead of fear, instead of manipulation, when Morris's face closes in on mine, I don't feel cornered or controlled.

I feel something else.

Seen.

"Baby, I want to kiss you. You want me too." It isn't a question, but he is giving me an out.

I don't want out.

I don't want to think.

I don't want to fear.

I *do* want Morris.

I don't wait for him to lead the way.

I lift my lips to touch his. The moment I tip my head back, I close my eyes and breathe in everything that is Morris. The woodsy, earthy smell of his skin. The rough friction of his beard against my chin. The softness of his lips as he claims mine, gently at first, as though he wants to sample every inch of my mouth slowly. The sweep of his lips against mine. Nudging me open with his tongue. The huff of his breath before he plunges his tongue deep into my mouth, tasting me, exploring me.

His hand snakes behind my neck and holds me. Keeping me close with a firm, loving hand.

Loving.

My body reacts to the kiss before my mind can catch up. I cling to Morris, holding his broad back with my hands. I press my hips to his, and a throttled groan escapes from between my lips.

He drinks in my mouth, feasting greedily. The kiss is deep, sensuous in a way I've only read about in books.

Passion like this is what people write love stories about.

Desire like this is how people get lost in each other.

Connection like this is how people fall in love.

Morris pulls back his head enough to take a breath, but he doesn't loosen the hand behind my neck. His other hand rests at the waistband of my yoga pants, his fingers dangerously close to my ass.

I want him to touch me. I want him to know what he's awakened in me, and I want to get lost forever in the bliss of that gritty chin scraping against my most tender skin.

I want Morris.

And he wants me.

And now we both know it.

He closes his eyes and rests his forehead against mine. He draws in a shaky breath, his chest rising with the effort, but he never moves his forehead from mine. "Alice Sparrow," he grits out, his voice husky with desire. "My beautiful little bird."

CHAPTER
ELEVEN
MORRIS

KISSING ALICE IS nothing like I expect. Kissing Alice is everything. She feels like hope and light, tastes like sex and sin, and sounds like laughter and home. All wrapped in one tiny, terrified package.

When I was hooking up with Jessica, the way her body seemed to crave my touch, how she rose up to meet me and gave every bit back in return, that was good.

But compared to this?

With Alice, shit… This is just *more*.

In the tiny bedroom of the apartment I rarely use, she shakes, trembling as I rest my forehead against hers.

"Baby, I want you to listen," I say, my voice low so Zoey can't hear. "We're in something now, me and you. You get that?"

Alice pulls her head away from mine so quickly, I feel a chill replace her sugar-scented warmth.

"What do you mean?" Her cheeks are stained pink, but the soft purple shadows under her eyes remind me she's still scared—and possibly in danger. "You and I are in what?" she asks, looking insecure and uncertain.

I motion to her with a finger. "Come here."

She does as I ask, so when she's close enough, I take her again in a kiss. But this time, I'm not going to leave room for any questions.

I hook a hand under her hair and the other under her ass and hoist her up so quickly, she wraps her legs around my waist on instinct.

I move us out of the line of sight of the open bedroom door and press her against the bedroom wall so I can support her weight. I lean against her body, letting her feel the full weight of what I'm feeling for her against her. My cock strains against the zipper of my jeans, begging for release. Just one kiss from the woman and my body is on fire, ravenous for the kind of satisfaction only Alice can bring.

Only Alice.

I consume her mouth with mine, shredding her delicate chin with mine. She gasps against me, but her body opens, softens, her desire for me meeting mine for her. She tightens her legs around my waist and claws at my back, my shoulders. My biceps are so huge beneath her hands, but I can still feel the way she explores my skin.

She's a wild one, this Alice. She nips at my lower lip, taking the lead and showing me how rough she likes it. I copy her movements, nibbling her lips and tasting the sugary tongue until we're both panting and breathless.

"Fuck," she says as I lower her to the floor.

"Can you stand?" I tease, a shit-eating smirk on my face.

"I can stand," she says, shaking her head in what looks like an erotic daze.

I lower my head to look in her eyes. "That," I say, motioning toward her. "On the bed, on the floor, against the wall. We're in *this* now. Feel me?"

Alice blinks and then laughs. "Oh, I felt you, all right." Her eyes fall to my waistband, and I can't help but adjust the rather inconvenient problem she's left me with.

"Darlin', just you wait."

Her eyes blaze dark brown then, the light-caramel color burned away by a husky, wanton fire.

"So…now what?" she asks. "I can't… You can't…" She falls quiet again and gets that worried, panicked look.

I'm gonna put a stop to that kind of thinking right fucking now. "I can," I say. "And you can, so we will."

I take her hand and lead her to the bed.

"Sit," I say. "Real talk."

Alice sits on the edge of my bed and tosses her sandy hair over a shoulder. "Morris, you don't want to get mixed up with me. You don't know…"

I give a look, and she clamps her lips closed. "All right now," I say. "Let's get a few things straight. Your marriage. You love him?"

Her eyes widen, and she immediately shakes her head, a hard, rapid *no*. "Morris, I don't think I ever loved him. He was convenient. He was capable. But love…" She sighs and looks down at her hands. "Let's just say, if I ever did, I haven't for a very, very long time."

"All right, then. Two more questions. Are you planning to divorce him?"

She nods. "The second, and I mean the very second, I can afford to serve him."

I nod at that and urge her on. "Last question. I'm in this. I don't know why, and I can't say for how long, but…" I toss a look toward the living room, where Zoey is laughing quietly along with the princess movie. "I'm in it. Are you?"

Alice follows my gaze and looks toward the living room. She flutters her eyes closed and takes a few shallow breaths. "I am," she says quietly.

"All right. That's all I need to know. Now, let's get into it. Who is this asshole husband, and what was on those messages that's got you so worked up?"

By the time Alice has explained the basics, I am ready to jump in anything I can find that moves and go kill that Jerry bastard myself.

Alice had spent more than two months putting together an escape. From her life. From her home. From her own goddamned husband.

She explained everything. About the beater car she bought because the SUV she drove was in the name of the dealership Jerry owned.

"If he called the police on me for stealing that car…" she said.

So, she bought a beater and a used kid's booster seat. Disabled location services on all of her devices. Left her daughter's iPad back in Miami on the floor of the SUV, and she came up with a plan to fake a spring break trip to visit her sister in Denver with Zoey.

"My sister knew we were never going to come, but she got a new puppy last week. She was planning on adopting one anyway, and she went ahead with it a little sooner. Zoey has always wanted a dog, but I could never swing the responsibility when Zoey was young. And then after Jerry… Well, let's just say I didn't think any animal deserved to be treated the way Jerry treated me."

Her words cut me to my core. The fact that Alice wouldn't put a dog through what she was going through at home made me want to take an electronic training collar and shock dear old Jerry's balls until he learned once and for all how to treat his old lady.

"What was your plan beyond getting away?" I ask. "Place to stay? Job?"

Alice meets my eyes. "Hotel for a night or two. Short-term rental. I figured I'd get a job waitressing pretty quick. Get Zoey in school. My sister promised to fly in and help me once we got through the first couple days. She's got some cash hidden for me that she was going to send later. The plan was for her to hold on to it for a week or so. Just in case."

"Just in case." I repeat that, and my blood boils under my skin. My fingers start itching, like I wanna claw right through the eyeballs of this Jerry motherfucker. But I'm not going to focus on that right now. I'll save what I want to do to this asshole for when I see him. Because if what Alice has told me is true—and I absolutely believe every word—I will be meeting this son of bitch sooner rather than later.

Alice and I are at the kitchen table, talking. Zoey fell asleep not long after the princess movie ended, and given how early she'd woken up for her spring break trip, Alice figured it would be better to let her sleep.

I liked that idea, so little ears wouldn't be as aware of our plans.

"So, you'll stay here," I tell her. "At least until your

car is ready. Where did you plan on landing? Were you headed to Daytona?"

Alice pinches her brows between two fingers. "Morris, I—"

I interrupt her by taking her hand away from her forehead and giving her a look. "In it," I remind her. "Now, go on. Where were you headed?"

She shakes her head. "Nowhere specific. My sister moved to Denver not long after our mom died, and I've been in Miami for most of my life."

"I'm sorry," I say. "About your mother."

Alice smiles, and it seems like the first real smile I've seen from her. "Thank you," she says. "I miss her. She died of breast cancer very, very young. She was only fifty-four."

"Fuuuuck," I hiss. "That is young. How long has it been?"

"Seven years," Alice says sadly. "She never knew I was pregnant with ZoZo." She worries a strand of her hair between her fingers. "In a way, I'm so, so glad. In fact, oddly, Zoey has a weird connection to my mom. I was waiting tables at the diner across from the car dealership. I'd finished my associate's degree, but I was trying to save up enough money to get a BA from a local college. Nothing crazy."

She meets my eyes and shrugs. "I was never one of those people who knew what I wanted to be when I grew up. My younger sister was the opposite. She was always so driven. She always had plans."

"What does she do in Denver?" I wonder.

"Technical writer," she explains. "She works for herself, lives on a small ranch out in kind of the middle of nowhere outside of Denver. Has a really small barn and a horse, a couple of cats. And, of course, the brand-new puppy."

I nod. "She on her own? No old man, no kids?"

"No." Alice grabs her phone and opens to the camera roll. "She was in a long-term relationship until about a year before Mom died. He lived in Denver. They met on a project. He worked at a pharmaceutical company in Denver and was project lead on an assignment. His company hired Rayne to work on the compliance manuals, and they fell for each other really fast. She lived here and he was in Denver, and she flew back and forth as often as she needed to for the project. But eventually, she ended up spending more and more time out there. They weren't going to go public with their relationship until the project ended, but…" Alice pressed her lips into a sad smile. "He passed away."

"What? What happened?"

"Terrible accident," she explained. "It was one of those weird cases where he went missing for a couple days. No one heard from him, he didn't show up to work. Nobody knew he and my sister were dating, so she was worried when she didn't hear from him, but she didn't know who else to call, what to do without outing their relationship. It all came out anyway. They found his body on the fourth day after he'd gone missing. Hiking accident. Seems like he went out alone and tumbled off a cliff."

"Fuck. Rotten luck."

Alice nodded. "And it gets even worse. She bought that small place outside of Denver right after Robert died. I don't know if she wanted to be close to the place he loved or what… Maybe she thought she'd keep it as a vacation home someday, but then Mom got sick and passed within just a few months. They found the cancer too late to do much."

"Alice…" I can't stand that this is my baby's story. So much pain. So much heartache. "So, your grieving sister moves away, you lose your mom, and then you get pregnant?"

Alice laughs, a harsh sound empty of any humor. "Exactly. I was careless for a while, dated around, drowned my sorrows in anything that masked the pain for a night. When I found out I was pregnant, the guy didn't even want to see me in person. He'd gotten a scholarship out of state, and the last thing he planned to do was support a family."

"You fight him for support?" I probably don't even need to ask. I can guess the answer.

Alice shakes her head slowly. "He knew he was the father. He knew what he was supposed to do. And he also knew that I was alone. My sister had moved away, Mom had passed. I was trying to stay sober long enough to wait tables and escape from the shitshow of my day-to-day life. How was I going to pursue him?"

"All right," I say, standing up. "I've heard enough about douchebag men. Make me a promise, yeah?" I lean over Alice and raise her chin with a finger.

"What's the promise?" she asks in a whisper.

My fingers itch to draw her close, to take her to my bedroom and fuck her senseless, worship her body until that look of sadness is replaced by absolute and utter bliss. But I can hear rustling on the couch that means Princess Zoey is waking up.

"Mama?" a sleepy, tiny voice calls.

"I'm in the kitchen, honey. I'm right here." Alice moves to stand, but I hold her arm and whisper in her ear as she heads out toward her daughter.

"Promise me," I hiss.

She waits for me to say the words. "Morris?" She looks at me with such trust, such blind, raw faith, it makes my chest ache.

"You're going to let me take care of you. At least until you can stand on your own feet."

The sweet trust collapses on her face, and those caramel eyes turn to stone. "I'm sorry, Morris. I just… can't." And then she turns away and heads toward her daughter.

CHAPTER
TWELVE
ALICE

THERE'S a loud knock at the door. Morris is up in a flash to answer it. I watch him as he checks who's there, and then he opens the door to let Leo back in.

"Hi, Leo," Zoey calls from the couch.

She straightens her dress and smooths her braid in a way that makes me grin. Leo is adorable. Handsome and sweet, if not a little on the young side. But he's perfectly crush-worthy for my six-year-old.

"Everything all right?" Morris asks, shutting the door behind him.

"Yeah, we're good." Leo is soaked with sweat and has oil stains on his jeans, but he's grinning. "I know you said to lock up your bike, but man, I couldn't leave it out there overnight. That place has been vacant for a while, but you just never know when somebody might break in. I put it on the trailer and drove it over. It's downstairs."

The look on Morris's face makes me fall a little bit in love with him. Falling in love. God. That reminds me of what he said right before Leo arrived. Letting Morris take care of me and falling in love with Morris are the last two things I should do. But somehow, I am pretty sure that no matter what I do, I won't have much choice in the matter.

"No shit. You did that?" Morris asks, sounding surprised.

"Yeah." Leo looks really proud of himself. "I have some news about the parts, too. I figured I'd bring you back the bike and let you know what I think I need. If you're still cool to lay out the cash, Alice's car doesn't really need that much."

They talk for a few minutes about the repair and the parts Leo thinks he can pick up from a local auto supply. Morris pulls a wad of bills from his wallet, and then they go downstairs to move Morris's bike.

He faces us before they leave. "I'll be right back," he says. "Just stay put."

As if we would go anyplace. As if we could. I just nod. "Thank you, Leo," I call quietly.

Leo lifts a hand and waves back at me and Zoey, who again calls goodbye to her crush.

"He's cute, isn't he?" I tease, nudging her in the ribs after they've left.

"Mama, stop!" Zoey giggles, kicking her feet and grabbing her side. "That tickles!"

"Oh, wait," I say. "Do you want me to stop

teasing you about Leo…? Or do you want me to stop *this*?" As I say that, I double down on the tickling and make sure to get a few extra finger-wiggles in the extra ticklish parts behind Zoey's knees.

"Mama!" she squeals, rolling and flopping on the couch like a little fish.

As we giggle and wrestle on the couch, the door opens, and Morris is back. His presence is so huge. He fills a room but doesn't darken it.

Somehow, his size is calming. Stabilizing. I look up at him, ready to meet his eyes, but the look on his face draws my attention back to Zoey.

She is frozen in place, staring at Morris as if she's been caught stealing. "I'm sorry, Morris," she says, her tiny voice reedy and thin. "I was being too loud."

I cover my face with my hands for a split second, ashamed that she's gone from playful and happy to scared and apologetic in a matter of seconds. And even more ashamed that, yet again, Morris is seeing that side of our lives. I don't know how I am going to be able to untrain the Jerry out of my daughter. But I don't have to wonder for long.

"You were being loud, princess?" Morris toes off his boots and leaves them in a pile by the door. "I don't think what I heard just now was loud. That was sort of like—who was that mouse sidekick in your princess dagger movie there?" He motions toward the TV, referring to the show she was watching earlier.

"Monty Mouse?" Zoey asks.

"That guy," Morris says, nodding. "Now, I seem to remember he made a teeny tiny squeak like this, 'Eeep, eeep, eeep.'"

I have to cover my mouth with a hand to keep from bursting into laughter. Hearing Morris imitate Monty Mouse is ridiculous. That tiny sound coming from that big, booming man.

Zoey seems to find it hysterical too, because she is giggling nearly uncontrollably, the shy, self-restrained little girl quickly driven away. "That sounds exactly like him! Morris is so good at voices!" Zoey cries.

"Morris is so good," I say before I can stop myself.

At the slight innuendo in my voice, Morris flicks a smoldering gaze at me. The man makes me hot just by looking at me.

"Well, now that my train of thought has completely derailed…" Morris looks at me. "What was I saying, princess? Oh yeah… Monty Mouse has this little voice, and that's what I heard from you just now. All those giggles?" He shakes his head and holds up a finger for her to watch and wait. "Those were just tiny noises. This—now, this is loud." Morris throws himself back on the couch and kicks his feet in the air. "Mommy, stop! Stop tickling me!" he booms. He's imitating Zoey as I tickled her, and the sight of this man, kicking and writhing and shouting, nearly undoes me.

Zoey is beside herself in a fit of raucous laughter. It's the most pristine and purest sound ever. Her little face is beet red, alight with freedom and silliness the likes of which I rarely get to see. The peals of her kid laughs are so sweet, so genuine. That's the girl I want Zoey to be every day. Loud and laughing and happy and free.

Morris keeps up the silliness, and I finally join in the laughter until tears stream down my cheeks.

"Now," Morris says, leaping up from the couch in an incredibly lithe movement. "That's the last I want to hear about overly good manners, apologies, and noise." He lowers his face to meet Zoey's. "I'm a casual guy, Princess Zoey," he explains. "You listen to your mama, you do as she says. But while you're here in my place, you can make noise, you can laugh... I don't care if you dance a kick line across the floor. Got it? Make yourself at home and relax."

Zoey looks at me, a small, subdued smile still on her face. I nod to reassure her it's okay. "Are we staying here, Mama? Are we staying with Morris?"

I look to Morris, who nods. "You sure are, little lady. We'll figure out the logistics."

He stands up and motions toward me.

I get up and join him in the kitchen.

"I'm going to make a quick run back to the compound," he says. "I'm going to swap out my bike for my truck so we can drive around with the booster seat."

I nod. "Do you want me to order anything for

later? Is there someplace we can walk and pick up groceries?"

Morris shakes his head. "Wait for me. We'll go together when I'm back. Won't be even an hour round trip." He looks past me to Zoey, who is fiddling with the remote, scrolling through the menu guide. "Will she be okay until I get back? You need something now?"

"No," I assure him. "She's okay."

"And you?" he presses. "I don't like how our conversation ended earlier. We're not done there."

I sigh. "I know." I nod at him. "I'm okay. Thanks."

"All right, then." He slides back into his boots and grabs his wallet and his phone. "Just wait here," he tells me.

He steps closer to me. So close that I can feel the heat radiating off his body. It's so cruel. So unfair.

Every cell in my body wants to sway forward and lean against this man. Find my place, my spot against his chest. How long will it be before he'll hold me again? Before he'll take me, press me against the wall, and kiss me like I'm the only thing left on earth he loves?

That's exactly the problem.

I can't let that happen.

Men are toxic.

Dependence on men is my fatal flaw.

There's no way in hell I'm getting stuck with some

other man—even a gorgeous, sexy, tattooed, gentle giant—while I'm still stuck under one of them.

Not now, maybe not ever.

Who knows.

My taste in men sucks.

My luck is even worse.

Maybe this is the time in my life I need to focus on doing something different.

"Alice." Morris's gaze sears my skin, and memories of his kisses, of his hand on my ass, make me wet even as we stand here in his kitchen. Fully clothed, inches apart... The power this man has over me makes me doubt this all the more.

"Yes?" I ask.

"Don't answer your phone for anyone but me, d'you hear?" His eyes are so dark now, I know he's serious. He's leaning forward, waiting for some acknowledgment that I've heard him. "Alice, don't answer your phone. Can you promise me that?" he asks.

I couldn't promise what he asked me before. That I'd let him take care of me. That I'd trust him, put myself and my daughter and all my failed hopes and dreams in his tattooed hands. I said no.

But this. Maybe this. Ignoring Jerry and not picking up the phone for one hour... Since it was what I'd planned on doing anyway, I don't see how it can hurt to agree.

But no matter what Morris says, it's not a promise.

It's not a promise to keep, anyway. It's common sense. I won't ever answer Jerry's calls again.

"I'll be fine," I assure him. "I won't answer the phone. I'll stay right here with Zoey until you're back. Then dinner." I try to brighten my tone a little, pull back some of the weight of my failures, my disappointments.

"Alice Sparrow," Morris says. He says my name like he's tasting it, savoring the shape of every letter on his tongue. The affection in his tone melts a little of my protective shell. But just a little.

"Morris…I don't even know your last name," I echo, trying to tease him, lighten the intensity of the energy radiating between us.

He gets the joke, and he grins. "Well, you're wrong there, little bird. Morris *is* my last name," he says, grabbing his keys and yanking open the door. He blows me a kiss, and I shake my head. "I'll be back as quick as I can," he says.

I lock the door behind him and then head to the window to see if I can watch him drive away. I can't. The apartment overlooks the rear of the building, and most of the parking is out front on the street. I listen for the sound of his bike, and find I'm inexplicably sad when I can't hear the roar of the muffler anymore.

CHAPTER
THIRTEEN
MORRIS

LEO LOOKS like a kid on his first trip to Disneyland when he pulls in behind me at the compound. I remember that enthusiasm, even though it was over two decades ago.

Leo seems like he's a sweeter kid than I ever was. Even with a junkie brother and who knows what was going on with his parents, he reminds me in a lot of ways of myself at his age: wide-eyed, enthusiastic, but at the same time, utterly lost. Belonging nowhere, to no one.

No family.

No real purpose.

Nothing but the clothes on his back and the desperation that drives young men out onto the road.

That's exactly how I felt so many years ago after losing my mom and escaping my father's wrath. It seemed like I'd lost everything.

My only family.

The roof over my head.

The journey brought me to my brothers and the Club. The president at the time didn't ask a single question. He gave me a room and a key, and before I knew it, this place was not just where I lived. It was home. The only place I could shut out memories of my mom.

No hospitals.

No medicine.

No nurses.

No bad news.

No sadness.

A different me.

When the Disciples took me in as a prospect, I was fortunate. Things were different back then.

Rougher.

A lot of clubs went down really dark paths over the years. Drugs, serious crime, trafficking. There were a lot of outlaw clubs, and when the Disciples found me, I was ripe. I so easily could've been led astray. Into hard shit, like whatever Leo's brother is on, no doubt. Meth, crack, smack, doing it, dealing it… Who knows.

Shit, I'm forty-five now.

I consider myself lucky that I don't wake up every morning in a prison-issue jumpsuit. It would have been so easy to go down that path.

But the MC gave me what it gave all my brothers.

Not just a place to land, but a place to stay. A place to belong.

A brotherhood that replaced whatever jacked-up family unit we'd left, lost, or had our asses kicked out of.

Leo parks his truck and looks over the exterior of the compound. "This is it?" he asks, his face barely hiding his awe.

"This is it," I confirm. I have a hard time not clapping the kid on the shoulder, so I do. "Come on. We got shit to do."

I head into the compound, but it's early evening and not many people are around.

"Well, well, look what the cat dragged in." Midge is standing in the kitchen, making something that literally smells like potato chip pie when we walk in.

"Midge." I greet her with a wink. I flirt with Midge to keep her happy, but I have to watch myself. She's liable to show up in my room thinking the wink was an invitation to more. I don't, and never will, go there. "This is Leo. He's helping me with the property we just picked up out east."

Midge clucks her tongue and looks Leo over.

I roll my eyes.

"Leo, Midge works for the club. Cleans, does some cooking." I motion to the oven and whatever that smell is. "If that's what you wanna call what's happening there."

"Fuck me, Morris," Midge says and means it.

"I'll take a rain check. Midge, sweetheart, you seen Tiny?"

Midge can be a handful, but she's around the compound so much, she knows most of the business and the comings and goings of my brothers.

She shakes her head. "Dunno."

I see my mistake and quickly move to fix it. "Leo, grab a couple beers from the fridge," I say.

Then I sidle up to Midge.

"Listen, beautiful," I say, looking her square in the eye. "Tiny was trying to reach me earlier today. You know where he is? I haven't heard from him." I give her a smile, laying on the sweetness.

She bends over and checks whatever that casserole thing is that's in the oven. "Kiss my ass, Morris. I'm not the boss of Tiny. I told you I don't know."

Leo is holding two beers like they're grenades that might blow up in his hands if he's too rough. I stifle the urge to laugh and slap them out of his hands. "They're just beers," I remind him. I grab one and twist the top off, then wave a hand to Midge as we leave. "You see Tiny, let him know I was here."

"Fuck you twice, Morris. And fuck your friend too." Midge watches us, eye-fucking Leo as we leave the kitchen.

"You're a dirty old woman, Midge," I call behind us, all but draining my beer.

"MILF to you!" she shouts.

Leo shakes his head, and his eyes are wide. "She

was…cool. Is she like a housemother or something?" He sips his beer as we head back through the compound toward the bedrooms.

I have to stop in my tracks and double over. I'm careful not to spill what's left of my beer as I rest a hand on my knees and wipe the tears from my eyes, I'm laughing so goddamn hard.

"No, son," I say, "Midge is the furthest thing from a mother you'll find."

The place is unusually empty and quiet, so I head over to my room, Leo following on my heels like an excited puppy.

He's asking me questions about everything he sees.

Are we all military veterans?

Are we criminals?

How do we make our money?

Do we work for the club?

Do we all live here?

"Okay, slow your roll, Diane Sawyer," I say, shoving open the door to my room.

"Who?" Leo asks, looking confused.

I chuckle. "News journalist, she was on TV," I explain. "Different clubs function in different ways. But only a handful of guys live here. Tiny's a full-timer, meaning he doesn't have an apartment or house or anyplace else to go."

"Doesn't he have a family?" Leo asks.

I shrug. "Used to have an old lady, but that ended ages ago. Most of the ones who stay here fly solo."

Leo nods again. "You alone, Morris? No wife or girlfriend?"

I chuckle. "No. Was never my style."

I head into my room and wave him in. He hovers at the doorway, taking in every inch of my space.

My room at the club is a little bigger than most. Since I'm the VP and stay here most of the time, I've got the largest space. And I keep it nice. Tiny's room, if we're being honest, looks like a hoarder's paradise within a couple hours of Midge cleaning. They are constantly at each other's throats. Tiny accumulating pizza boxes and beer cans and food wrappers, Midge cleaning up after him and mocking him for not eating the "home-cooked" meals she makes and stashes in the fridge.

A man of Tiny's stature has to put in the time to earn that nickname. He'd need a dumpster full of Midge's pies to stay as big as he does. Although, to be fair, the dumpster is about the only place I'd ever put Midge's cooking.

I open the top drawer of my dresser and pull out the key to a lockbox, then motion for Leo to give me some privacy while I pull the lockbox from its hiding place.

I've got no secrets from my brothers in the club. They know where every penny I own is stashed, where I keep the weed I every so often like to light up, and everything in between. And I like this kid, but trust is another thing altogether.

"What about…" Leo pauses. "Alice?"

"What about Alice?" I echo.

He nods and stuffs the cash I just gave him for the parts he'll need to get for Alice's car in his pocket. "Seems like, I don't know. I thought she was your girlfriend or something. You guys seem like you've been together a long time."

I raise a brow at him. "I've known the woman since this morning. Met her at a gas station."

Leo's eyes widen. "Wait…what? Are you serious?"

I nod.

"Morris, what the fuck, man? You're going to all this trouble for someone you don't even know?"

I level him with a look. "I just told you. I've known her since this morning."

If the look on his face is any indication, Leo catches the warning in my voice. "Right. Right. Sorry, man. I mean, Morris, I…didn't mean any disrespect. You two just seem like you have something. I thought…"

"Never said we didn't have something."

I let that sink in, and it does quicker than I thought.

"So, okay. Right." Leo nods, looking like he's still thinking it all over, but processing it. "So, you like her…"

I snap my lockbox closed, secure the lock, and

motion for Leo to turn away. I secure the box in its hiding place.

"Why I'm doing this," I say, "is Jerry Cruz."

Leo shrugs. "Whozzat? Should I know who that is?" He pulls out his phone and Googles the name. "Cruise like Tom Cruise?"

I shrug. "Car dealer in Miami." I don't know how to spell that fuckwad's name, and I don't want to. "He's why Alice and Zoey are on the run."

"Found him." Leo holds up his phone to show me. "Looks like a Class-A douchebag if I've ever seen one."

I can't resist the urge to put a face to the name. When I look, I'm not at all surprised to see a face that I will fantasize about smashing with my bare fists for a long time.

"He looks like a dickwad. I can't picture Alice with a guy like this," Leo says.

"Assholes come in all shapes and sizes," I say.

I just knew that whatever drew Alice to this shit-eater in the first place—desperation, his persistence, who knows—the kind of modern-day marriage of convenience they ended up with was all that was left.

"Come on," I say. "We got people to feed."

Leo nods and takes one last look around my room. I have a hand-sewn quilt of the American flag hanging over my bed.

"What's that?" Leo asks, motioning to the quilt above my bed.

"Mom," I say simply. "She was a quilter. Up until the day she passed."

"No shit…" Leo walks closer to inspect it. "She made this?" he asks. "That's unbelievable, Morris. Really talented woman. I'm so sorry for your loss."

"Hand-done," I explain. I don't expect him to appreciate the skills my mom had.

Hand-sewing every quilted square, cutting every scrap of fabric by hand. She never owned a sewing machine, and even though I bought her one the first chance I got, she donated it. Gave it to a friend in her quilting circle when her old-ass Walmart Singer finally took a shit.

"Mom was an artist at heart. She made beauty with her hands. Loved to work fabric like it was her canvas. That's why I hang a lot of the quilts she made. Got one back at the apartment. In my bedroom over the bed."

"Holy shit," Leo says, his voice appropriately low with awe. "How long did that take her? Did she only make like two in her whole life? That must have taken forever!"

I hesitate and check the time. I still haven't seen or heard from Tiny, and I want to get back to Alice and the kid, but Leo's questions have got me thinking.

"Check this out." I kneel on the floor and pull a custom-built cedar box from under the bed. Inside are four quilts my mom made. "These are the ones I don't use," I explain.

"Girl colors," Leo supplies.

I laugh. "Well, that's not how I would have described it, but yeah." The quilts I keep stored are the ones my mom made but hadn't given away when she died.

When I open that bin, a slight whiff of air greets me, and even though I know it can't be true, I swear I smell my mom in that moment. The quilts have been cleaned since Mom passed, but somehow being close to these things makes me feel her presence.

"Zoey would freak," Leo says, pointing to the quilt on the bottom. "Blue flowers, like her princess dress."

I look at the quilt he's pointing to. It's an unusual color combination of light turquoise, yellow, and a pale baby blue, just like the color of Zoey's dress. "Grab 'em," I say, yanking the plastic from the cedar chest. I hand Leo the wardrobe-style bag and shove the empty crate back under my bed.

He looks at me. "What're we doing?"

"We need more blankets at the apartment," I say. "No use letting clean quilts just sit here. Now take 'em before I change my mind."

Leo doesn't say a word but hangs on to the bag like I ask.

I take a last look around my room for anything else I might need. There's no question I am going to stay at the apartment tonight with Alice and Zoey, so I grab a pillow off my bed and throw some shit in a leather backpack.

"Grab the keys on the wall over there, would you? The spare keys to the apartment have the bottle opener for a key chain." My cell phone's buzzing, so I point toward the keys and look who's calling.

"Alice? Everything all right?" I hold the phone in tense fingers.

"Morris…" Alice's voice is a whisper. "There's someone here. There's a man at the door."

"Is it Cruz?" I bark, motioning to Leo to pick up the pace. "Is it your husband?"

"I don't know him," she says. Then over the line, I can hear a loud knocking. "Morris…"

"Don't open the door, no matter what. You hear me?" I grab my backpack and sling it over my shoulder. "We're on our way. Do not open that door, and if anything happens, you call 9-1-1, then me. You got that?"

"Hurry, Morris," Alice whispers. "Hurry, baby, please."

If I weren't feeling the adrenaline and the need to tear the fuck outta there, I would spend more time appreciating that she called me baby. "Leo," I bark. "Key. We gotta roll now. Someone's pounding on my apartment door."

"Oh shit." Leo looks concerned. "But, Morris…"

"Keys. Come on, kid. We gotta go!"

"Morris!" The tone in Leo's voice has me looking his direction. "The keys aren't here. No keys with a bottle opener attached."

"Let me look." I shove past him and look over the row of hooks with neatly hung spare keys on the wall. "God fucking damn it."

There aren't enough curses in my goddamn vocabulary for this. Every hook on that wall holds exactly what it's supposed to. Every key is in its place.

Every key, that is, except the spare key to my apartment.

CHAPTER
FOURTEEN
ALICE

"ZOEY." I keep my voice low and calm. "Let's go into Morris's bedroom. I want to show you a quilt he has on the wall. It's really pretty. Come on."

Zoey's eyes are wide, and she looks as terrified as I feel. "Mama, who's at the door? Where's Morris?"

"He's coming, baby. Don't worry. Now come on."

I leave the volume on the TV where it is, hoping the noise of the show Zoey was watching muffles the sounds of our voices and movements.

As we head back toward Morris's bedroom, I hear another loud series of knocks on the door.

"Come on," I urge, hustling Zoey into the bedroom. I close the door quietly behind us and twist the tiny doorknob lock. It won't keep out much, but it will give me a few extra minutes to call 9-1-1 if we need to.

Zoey starts to cry quietly. "I'm scared, Mommy. What's happening?"

"Honey, I don't want you to be scared." I sit her down on Morris's bed and put my hands on her shoulders. "Listen to me. I'm going to take care of you. Nothing bad is going to happen."

Even as I say it, I hope like hell it's true. I never, ever want to have to lie to my daughter again.

I look around the room for anything I can use as a weapon. A man like Morris has to have a baseball bat or something I can use to defend us.

"Just be quiet for Mommy, okay, honey?" I start looking through the room as quietly as I can, but it's too late. I hear a sound that freezes the blood in my veins.

The unmistakable sound of the front door swinging open and closing shut.

I reach for my cell phone, swiping across the touchscreen as I debate calling 9-1-1.

Goddamn it.

I realize I don't know the address where we are. I don't know what to tell them or how to tell them to find us. Morris is on his way, but I have no idea how far away he is or how long it will take him to get back here.

My heart is pounding so hard I can hardly hear, but when Zoey leaps up off the bed, I reach for her.

"Shh!" I shake my head and grab her, holding her close, my phone still in one hand.

"Mama…they have dogs!"

Completely gone is the terrified look on Zoey's face. In its place is pure delight. My baby adores puppies, dogs, pretty much all animals. That was part of how we convinced Jerry to let us go on spring break.

My sister adopting that brand-new puppy was enough to excite Zoey for weeks. I convinced Jerry that since we were never going to get her a pet—his rules—that she could get her fill on a trip out to see her aunt.

"What? Dogs?"

I set down my phone and listen. I can only make out movement at first, noises that sound like running, and shoes scuffing against the floor.

And…barking.

"What the fuck, Morris? Come out here, asshole. I don't have time to play your dumb-ass games."

Someone in the apartment is cursing a blue streak, talking to Morris as though they think he's here.

I hear voices from behind the door and more running sounds. Then suddenly, someone is at the bedroom door, twisting the knob, but it's locked.

"I don't care if you're balls deep in a bitch. I need you, man."

I take a deep breath. The man on the other side of the door is not Jerry.

Suddenly, the man is pounding on the bedroom

door. "Morris, you nasty fucker! Get your ass out here."

I hold a finger to my lips for Zoey to stay quiet. I have her stand right behind me, and I hold her body securely with one arm while I unlock the bedroom door. I pull the door open and jump back to put a little extra distance between myself and the stranger.

I look up, and my eyes meet a tuft of chest hair that looks like a gnarled-up bird's nest. "Morris isn't here," I say, taking two steps back, moving my daughter with me.

The man fills the doorway of Morris's bedroom. He is, if it's even possible, more enormous than Morris. He's as wide as he is tall, and his head nearly brushes the doorframe. He's wearing a V-neck gray T-shirt over his bowling-ball belly, but I recognize the leather vest as the same exact type Morris has.

"I'm Alice," I say, meeting his eyes with a steady look. "And this is Zoey."

"Holyyyyyyy shit," he mutters. The man's mouth sags open.

I see him look from me to Zoey, from Zoey to me, and then repeat the whole thing, like he can't believe what he's seeing.

He wipes his hand on his sagging black jeans and holds it out to me. "Er… Hi. I'm Tiny," he says.

Well, of course, he is.

Zoey is lying on the floor in the middle of Morris's apartment, literally at the bottom of a pile of puppies, when Morris storms through the door.

Two of the dogs race for him and start yapping and barking at his ankles, while the tiny one takes the opportunity to hog all of Zoey's attention, covering her face in licks and kisses.

"What in the name of…" Morris looks down at the dogs, up at me, over toward Zoey, and then a look of comprehension overtakes his face. "Tiny."

Morris crosses the room toward his friend, who's sitting with an ankle propped up on a tree-trunk–like leg, watching the scene unfold.

"You mother…fudger." Morris holds a hand out to his friend and hauls his ass off the couch.

They do a one-armed man hug, and Tiny shakes his head. "Tried to reach you all day, man. I had a little…situation." Tiny looks at me and the woman who belongs with all these dogs.

"'S'all right," Morris says. "You took the spare key?"

Tiny nods. "Figured you wouldn't mind, brother, but again… Didn't know you had shit going on."

"Stuff," Morris corrects, pointing to Zoey.

Morris crosses the room to me, and when he does, I am so relieved to see him, I grab him in a hug.

"So, we met Tiny," I explain. "And Lia."

"And the dogs!" Zoey calls, leaping up from the

floor and smoothing down her dress. "Hi, Morris. Hi, Leo."

Leo is hovering in the doorway, looking thoroughly confused. "Hi, Zoey," he says. "Everybody's all right?"

I nod.

"You sure?" he asks.

Morris hasn't released me yet, and I stay close, savoring his heat. "We're fine," I say. "Tiny and I have been chatting a bit, and Zoey is really excited about the dogs."

"I think I'm almost caught up," Morris says, looking over at the young woman on the couch beside Tiny, who's sat back down. "But you want to fill me in?"

Tiny looks sheepish as he peers over at the woman beside him.

The young woman is totally engrossed in her phone. She's dressed like she's just back from a weekend-long music festival. She has feathers braided into her long hair, and her bare feet are tucked under her, each toenail painted a different color. Each fingernail has teeny tiny, half-peeled stickers on them, and she's wearing earrings that travel the entire ridge of each ear.

"Um, yeah. So, Morris…" Tiny scoots forward on the couch, grabbing the waistband of his black jeans and holding them up as he stands. "This is Lia."

At the sound of her name, the girl's head pops up.

She gives Morris the same sunshine smile she gave Zoey and me earlier. "Hiya!" she says, and I half expect her to pop a piece of gum, she's so perky. "Thanks for helping me out. My dad wasn't sure if your apartment allows dogs, but I know I can't stay with my girl crew at the compound. So yeah, I'm like, so super psyched to meet you!"

Morris's mouth drops open for just a moment, and then I see a tiny curl of amusement at the corner of his lips. "Your dad? Your girl crew?" he repeats.

Tiny huffs a deep breath and points toward his own chest. "Dad," he clarifies. Then he points to the three dogs who have now climbed onto the couch and circled Lia. "Girl crew."

Morris looks as if he's going to rupture something. He's holding back laughter or shock, but I can't tell which.

"Walk me through this. Someone?" He looks from Tiny to me, but I know about as much as Morris does at this point.

Tiny walks up to his friend and puts a hand on his shoulder. "So, Morris, I'd like you to meet my daughter, Lia Dove."

"That's my whole first name, but you can call me Lia," she offers, popping up from the couch. She pads over to Morris on bare feet. An armload of bracelets jangles as she holds out her hand with the colorful nails toward him like he's not this enormous, tattooed biker. "My mom was a hippie. Total hippie," she says, laughing. "But in the best kinda way. Dad didn't know about me until what, Dad, like, a couple months ago?"

"Something like that," Tiny mutters. He's looking really embarrassed, shuffling from foot to foot.

Morris, for his part, holds out his hand, now appearing completely unfazed. "Nice to meet you, Lia." He looks down at the girl crew. "And your mother is…?"

"Oh, Mom is fine," she says. "She's actually, like, great. She met this billionaire or something. She's, like, living on his yacht. And… Oh, well, I guess I don't know. She's off having her second youth, and I just got the heck out of the way."

Lia walks up to Tiny and slips an arm around the big man's waist. It's laughable watching her petite, thin arm snake just a fraction of the way around Tiny.

"Poor Dad here didn't even know about me until…"

"Wasn't too long ago," Tiny mutters under his breath. "Total clusterfuck. A good clusterfuck, but still a clusterfuck."

"What about…" Morris starts to ask until Tiny shakes his head ever so slightly.

"Haven't gotten that far," Tiny replies. "Shit's still unfolding."

"Sounds like it's hung up, brother. There's nothing left to unfold."

I'm so confused and doing my best to keep up with their conversation as they dance around something.

"I know about my sister," Lia adds, making things clear. "Dad says I should wait to give her some time to deal with her feelings."

"Right, sweetheart. She's not as—" he pauses, rubbing the back of his neck "—sweet as you. She'll calm down after she has some time to think."

Morris laughs, running his hand over his mouth to cover the subtle movement. "Sure," he mutters.

"So, you see," Tiny supplies, moving beyond the talk of his other daughter. "Lia here needs a place to crash. Her mom…the uh, girlfriend I had twenty years ago…"

"Twenty-three," Lia corrects. "I'm twenty-two now, so if you factor in gestation, you know, Dad and Mom hooked up like twenty-three years ago. And it's okay, Dad. We're all adults here." She peeks over at Zoey and then holds a hand over her mouth. "Almost all of us," she whispers. "Mom had a one-night stand with Dad and didn't know how to find him," she whispers, keeping an eye on Zoey. Then she raises her voice to normal speaking volume as she resumes the story where Tiny left off. "So yeah. Mom, Dad's *girlfriend* from way back, moved to Canada with her richie rich new man. She sold her townhouse, and I packed up and hit the road with my girl crew."

Tiny points to the dogs.

"Yeah." Morris nods. "Got that much."

"It took some doing, but I found my dad, spent a couple months on the road in my van, and here we are! Reunited!" Lia wraps her arms around Tiny's stomach and holds him tight.

"Well, that's… That's wonderful," Morris says, looking confused.

"We were kind of hoping Lia and the dogs could crash here for a few days," Tiny says. "I talked to Lia's mom this morning—"

"Jen," Lia fills in. "Mom's name is Jen." Lia drops to the carpet beside Zoey and picks up one of the dogs. They chatter and play, Lia showing my daughter how she painted one of her dog's nails.

While they make a fuss over the dogs, Leo watches, seemingly awestruck by Lia.

"Come in, son," Morris says, motioning for him to stop hovering in the doorway. "This is Leo," he calls out.

He gestures for Tiny and me to join him in the kitchen. The apartment is small and open, so we keep our voices low so we're not overheard.

"What the hell, man?" Morris asks. But he's grinning like a loon.

"Goddammit, Morris." Tiny is flushed a deep red, and he's fidgeting. "Been tryin' to reach you all day. I didn't know what the fuck to do! She has three dogs, Morris. Dogs!"

I cover my mouth with my hand to avoid bursting into laughter.

"All right. A couple things. You sure she's yours? This ain't some scam?" Morris asks.

"Nah." Tiny shakes his head. "It's legit. I was contacted by a PI a few months ago, but I thought they were working on some criminal shit. You know I don't talk to cops, man. You know the trouble I got into a while back. I figured my past could stay buried if I just didn't answer, but then I get this call from Jen out of nowhere." I can feel the huff of Tiny's sigh from two feet away.

"It wasn't really just this morning," he goes on. "She really is my kid. Jen and I hooked up at a bar years ago when I was a prospect. She only knew my real first name, the one I went by before I was patched in. She knew I was a biker, but I didn't have a patch or anything yet, and she could never remember the name of the club."

"She raised Lia all these years by herself?" I ask.

Lia seems like a completely untraumatized, lively, beautiful young woman. If this Jen woman could do it… Well, I already know that I have to. It's just encouraging to see at least one example close by of someone who has.

"Yeah," Tiny nods. "That's why the kid's here. I mean, my daughter. Her. Lia. Lia." Tiny looks like he is still struggling to feel his way through the names and terms. "Jen was a nurse when I met her, and I guess she married some high-up guy at a pharma company and took off. Lia thought it'd be the perfect time to find her birth father."

"And she just showed up in your life this morning?" I can't imagine just showing up on the doorstep of a man I've never met, expecting to be treated like family.

I pretty much dropped into Morris's life, and here he is, treating me better than I deserve.

Better than my husband.

Better than my boyfriend before that.

Better than anyone, honestly.

Morris is taking care of me. He is there for me. And for reasons I don't fully understand.

It hardly makes sense. And yet, here we are.

"Not exactly," Tiny admits. "The girl and I have been in touch for months. Nothing big, just e-mail, some calls. I knew she wanted to meet up, to come out this way, but she's…kind of a free spirit, if you know what I mean. She didn't really give me specifics. Like a date."

He looks over at her, chattering away with her dogs and Zoey. "But I'm glad she's here. A call to let me know she was coming would have been nice, but… I guess that's family."

"Well, congratulations, Dad," Morris says. "You're now the proud father of a girl crew."

Tiny gives Morris a fist in the gut, but it lands softly. "Asshole," he mutters. "So, can she crash here or what? I can't have all that…in my room at the compound."

Morris watches Lia, who is wriggling around on her belly on the floor with Zoey, doing God only knows what.

The dogs seem to know this game well, and they follow her movements with poses of their own.

Leo, for his part, seems transfixed by the hippie beauty. He's moved to the kitchen with the adults, seemingly curious about what's going on.

"No dogs allowed here, Tiny," Morris says, shaking his head. "Wish I could help a brother out, but apartment rules."

"Goddammit," Tiny says. "Yeah, I got it. It's all right. We'll figure something out."

"She can stay with me," Leo offers.

All eyes in the kitchen fly to the kid.

"I mean, I have a house with a yard. Three bedrooms, two bathrooms." Leo shrugs. "My brother's been MIA for a year, since the legal action started on the shop. I've got room. Don't mind the dogs."

Tiny cocks his head, and I see him thinking it over. I step back from the guys to let them sort out their issues. It's like the guys are a fraternity, not a motorcycle club. I keep that thought to myself because I don't think Morris would much appreciate the comparison. But if you count the dogs, the girl crew outnumbers the bikers.

Before anyone can respond, my phone buzzes with a text message. I check my phone and see I have five messages already, more texts coming in fast and furious. I scan the messages from my sister.

Rayne: Alice, he knows.

Rayne: Alice, are you okay? Are you getting my texts? He knows, Alice.

Rayne: Alice, call me as soon as you get this.

Rayne: I'm scared, Alice. Jerry's been calling me every five minutes. He won't stop calling.

Rayne: God, I'm scared. Please, big sis, call me as soon as you can.

Rayne: Do you think he'd come out here? Come to Denver? Does he have my address, Alice?

I hold the phone in shaking hands as I walk up to Morris.

"Baby?" He looks away from the conversation he is having with Tiny and Leo. "What is it?"

My pulse turns to lead as I hold up the phone and show him Jerry's text.

Jerry: I thought the dog you were going to see was your sister's. Not three yapping mutts.

"Jerry's watching us right now," I say before the room goes black.

CHAPTER
FIFTEEN
ALICE

"SHE'S gonna be just fine, aren't you?" A perky, happy voice I don't recognize finds me through the haze.

I struggle weakly to open my eyes until I feel Zoey's little hand in mine.

"Mommy, what happened? Did you fall?"

"She's okay, little love. Your mama's okay. Let's just let her sip some water."

I sit up and realize I'm on a kitchen chair, surrounded by Lia, Zoey, and Morris.

Morris is holding my phone, and his face is red with a rage I haven't seen since he found us at the side of the road with the stranger.

"Here you go." Lia hands me a glass of cold water. "I would add some herbal remedies, but all my stuff is out in Dad's truck."

"I'm all right, thank you." I take a sip and squeeze

Zoey's hand. "Go ahead and play with the puppies, baby. Mommy's fine. I just felt a little light-headed."

Zoey gives me a hug. "Okay, love you." She kisses my cheek and then bounces back into the living area. "Lia, can the puppies have treats?"

"Well, of course, they can have treats," Lia tells Zoey.

Morris comes to sit beside me and places his hand over mine. "I put your sister's number in my phone. I texted her that you're with me and she's not to answer any calls from that motherfucker. I told her I'll have you call her and to not, under any circumstances, give my number to anyone."

I nod. "Okay, who did you tell her you were?"

"Your boyfriend." His answer makes the room start to spin again, but then I focus on the salt-and-pepper of his beard. The strength of his grip on my hand. Morris leans close and whispers in my ear, "We need to get you out of here. Do you have all the numbers you need from this phone? Is there anyone you need to be able to reach?"

"My sister. Just a few friends, but no one I need right now. Anyone I need to reach, I can e-mail in a few weeks."

"Okay." He looks me in the eye. "Baby, this phone's gotta go. He's tracking you."

No, he can't be.

I shake my head again, fear and confusion warring for control over my thoughts. "That's not possible. I disabled location services on my phone. There's no way he can find me with it."

Morris presses his lips into a thin line. "Baby, who bought the phone? When it was new? You or him?"

"We got new phones together," I explain. "Why?"

"Who set them up? Do you have a family plan, a shared account?"

"Well, yeah." I struggle to remember. The phone is almost a year old now, so not *new*. "Jerry's business paid for all the accounts. Our cars were titled to the business. That's why I didn't take his SUV. He could have reported it stolen and called the cops. It wasn't in my name, so I had no rights to it."

Morris nods. "Baby, it's possible he's installed something on your phone. It's not at all uncommon. Spouses use apps that you'd never know are on the device to track where their partner is. If you're not where you say you are, he probably knows to within a couple of blocks exactly where you are. He knew the minute you didn't get on that plane this morning."

"No." I drop my face in my hands. "How? How do you know? How's that possible?"

"I told him," Leo says. He comes closer to us and lowers his head to explain. "Sorry, Alice. Morris isn't as tech-savvy as you probably are." He gives Morris a smile, but Morris just lifts a brow in silent warning.

"I'm not," I admitted. "But I checked the phone plan before I left. I didn't see anything on there that would make me think Jerry did anything to the account."

"If there is something on the phone itself, it's likely not on the account," Leo explains sweetly. He points to the phone. "Invisible apps. It could be anything. No way to know for sure without some kind of tech specialist. There are so many ways to chase down a cheating spouse, a lying teenager. I mean, parents use all kinds of tricks to keep track of their kids without the kids knowing about it. Can you imagine all the ways you can do the same thing for a spouse?"

"And I'd never see it? I wouldn't even know it was on the phone?" I ask.

Goddammit all to fucking hell.

I'm an idiot.

"Don't feel bad about it, Alice," Leo says, trying to be positive. "It's a really specialized thing. It's not like you can just hop on to Facebook and see ads for spouse-stalking apps. And if you're an honest person, which I totally know you are, you'd never even think to use something like this."

I nod. That much, at least, is true.

"The technology will come in handy when Zoey's a teenager," Leo says with a lighthearted grin, but Morris shoots him a look, and Leo backs away and stands near Tiny.

"So, what do we do?" I ask Morris. "Jerry knows

I'm here. He's seen me. He might even be right outside. Right now."

I feel sick, and the room swims again before my eyes.

"Alice!" Morris grabs my arms and brings me to standing. "We're going to get out of here. We're going to go someplace Jerry can't find you. And I sure as hell hope that asshole is outside. I'll end this right here, right now."

"No, no," I say. "Just, please…" I put a palm on his arm and slide it down to his hand. I lace my fingers through his and squeeze. "What are we going to do? Do you have a plan?"

Morris nods. Without releasing my hand, he grabs my phone off the table. "We start with this," he says, then drops it on the kitchen floor, and with a single stomp of his boot, the phone shatters into a million pieces.

CHAPTER
SIXTEEN
MORRIS

"MOM, please, please! Please can I have a sleepover with the doggies, please!" Zoey is in her pajamas and has freshly painted toenails.

Lia is also in pajamas, if you count fringed pants and a tank top that has more cutouts than fabric sleepwear. She's sitting with her feet spread out in front of her, and she's fanning her damp toes with an old, beat-up issue of *Hot Rod* magazine she found in a pile on a coffee table.

"Can we pleeeeease!" Lia giggles and imitates Zoey, calling out so her voice carries past me and into the kitchen.

Somehow, there is a motley crew of bikers, women, dogs, and children in Leo's house.

I look over at him apologetically. "Leo's house, Leo's rules," I say.

If he doesn't mind all these strangers in his house,

I can't imagine why he'd care if this girl crew sleeps on the floor.

Leo is helping Alice put away the dishes and clean up the dinner table. We ordered takeout for dinner, and after Lia went through a shockingly complex ritual to prep her dogs' food, everyone in the house had eaten.

Tiny is finishing off a beer on the couch, watching his daughter and Alice's daughter add the finishing touches to a living room floor pedicure, while the dogs crash out in various spots on the furniture, stuffed from their meal of whatever that shit was with herbal supplements Lia decided to feed them.

Leo looks back at me. "Morris, whatever, man. I'm easy. Mi casa, as they say."

I don't want to make myself at home in another man's house, but he has three bedrooms, and we have Alice, Zoey, and Lia, as well as myself, to settle someplace for the night. Tiny plans to head back to the compound to sleep in his own room tonight, which solves one of the bedroom questions.

"You sure you'll be all right if I head out, man? This is all good?"

I've known Tiny a long time, and my brother looks fucking beat. If I became a hands-on father like this all in one day, I'd want to retreat to my room at the compound too.

Then again, maybe not.

I watch Zoey giggle and play with Lia. The little

girl seems like she's chilling out right in front of my eyes. As if just a few hours out from under the clutches of her mother's douchebag husband were releasing all the chains that kept the kid toeing the line like a soldier. I could be done with this mess in the morning. Let Leo deal with the car and let Alice sort out her own business with her ex.

Go right back to the life I thought I had yesterday. But I know there's no way I can go back now. Something changed when I found Alice in that gas station. The new building. Jessica moving on, ending things for good. I don't think I could deny how I'm feeling, even if I tried.

I wouldn't dream of walking away from these two now. Alice and Zoey.

Not tonight.

Not now.

Not ever.

Tiny hauls himself off the couch and waits.

"Yeah," I assure Tiny. "Yeah, we're all good. Come on back in the morning if you want. You can check out the new property. Take your daughter for breakfast."

"I will," he says. Then he heads over to Leo. "Thanks, man. You're saving my ass."

"Thank you for dinner and the beer," Leo says, turning to clap Tiny's hand in a shake. "Happy to host your daughter as long as you need."

Oh, Leo, the poor fucker.

He's got no game.

He can't keep his eyes off Tiny's daughter, but I can't tell if she's even noticed Leo's alive.

Lia is a sweet one, but she's got one foot on another plane. She's more connected with kids and animals than other adults.

Although, she did a great job helping when Alice had her little anxiety spell back at my apartment. Growing up with a nurse for a mother rubbed off somewhat, it seems.

Tiny walks through the mess of tissues and nail polish, dog toys and pillows, to wish his daughter goodnight.

"I'll be going, then," he says stiffly.

"Oh! Dad, wait up! Wet nails, I gotta move slow. Don't leave!" Lia leaps to her feet, dramatically spreading her toes and moving in a zombie-like walk toward Tiny. "Ooooohhhhh, I'm so happy!" Lia circles her dad's enormous belly, reaching her arms as far around him as they can go.

Tiny gives the girl the world's most awkward hug, barely patting her back with a hand before frowning and stepping away from her.

"All right, then. You got money? You need food or something?" Tiny asks.

"Aw, look at you!" Lia reaches up and pinches Tiny's cheek, being careful to hold her fingers out so she doesn't smear her nails. "Such a dad. I'm great! Got everything I need right here." She pats her chest, and I swear Tiny rolls his eyes but then quickly composes himself.

"Right, then. Right, okay. Okay." Tiny stands there muttering to himself, so I wave him off.

"Come on. I'll walk you out. I wanna lock up." I head toward the front door with Tiny close on my heels.

We step outside into the humid night air. Darkness has fallen, but Leo's motion-activated exterior lights turn on once we get past the front door.

"What the fuck, man," Tiny says. "I need a smoke."

"Go home and smoke a j," I say. "Been a day."

Tiny nods. "This Alice…" He doesn't finish the sentence. He doesn't need to.

I nod back.

"Okay." Tiny gets it. "We weren't followed, and without that phone, that fucker of an ex shouldn't be able to find her, right?"

"That's the hope," I say.

"Thanks for bailing me out of a tight one," he says.

"'S'all right."

Truth be told, I think having Lia and those yapping dogs will be good for Zoey. Leo sure as hell doesn't seem to mind, and keeping our host happy is a win-win.

"Tomorrow, then," Tiny says. "I'll put the key to

your place back at the compound? Or you want it now?"

"I'll take it," I say, and I grab it when he hands it my way. "May need some shit from over there at some point."

Tiny claps me on the back and then climbs behind the wheel of his truck.

I wait until his taillights are out of sight before I walk the perimeter of Leo's house.

It's a classic split ranch built on a slab, but I don't like the fact that any asshole with a hammer could get in without so much as a stepladder. The backyard is fenced, but the fence is old as fuck. It's clear that no one has put any money into keeping this place up in some time. But it's a roof over our heads, and tonight, I'll be within arm's reach of Alice and Zoey.

I'll be able to keep them safe.

When I go back inside, I flip the deadbolt lock on both the screen door and the aluminum exterior door. The front door opens right into the living room, which has, in the few minutes I've been gone, been transformed into a sleepover wonderland.

Zoey and Lia are lying on the floor with their backs leaned against the couch, tucked beneath my mother's quilts.

The dogs, two tiny critters that can't weigh more than fifteen pounds together, and then a medium-sized dog that looks like a mix of golden retriever and German shepherd, are passed out cold around them.

Zoey, leaning against the couch, my mother's quilt over her lap, gives me pause. Lia is young enough to be my daughter, and of course, so is Zoey. Even with the age gap, the two could be sisters.

Leo is lying on the couch behind Lia and Zoey, transfixed by the feathers in Lia's braids when he's not watching the kids movie playing on the TV.

But it's not until I see Alice that something catches in my chest. She's sitting alone at the kitchen table. She's taken off her shoes, and her feet are bare. Her legs are crossed, and she's sipping a beer, watching me intently. There is something in her eyes, a look that draws me in, toward her.

I head into the kitchen, fill two glasses with water, and set one on the table in front of her.

"You know we just did all the dishes," she teases.

I stand behind her and put my hands on her shoulders. "You sure did," I note.

"Morris," she starts, but I squeeze her shoulders. She looks up at me, and I shake my head.

"Let's take a minute," I say.

"For what?" she asks.

I don't say the word on the tip of my tongue, so I just fall silent.

Home.

I want to take a minute to savor something I have not felt since my mom passed.

What it feels like to be home.

CHAPTER
SEVENTEEN
ALICE

I CRAWL on my knees through a mess of dogs and blankets and pillows to get to my daughter. "Did you brush your teeth good?" I ask.

"Lia watched. Tell her," Zoey says, nodding vigorously.

"She did absolutely great," Lia yawns big, revealing her perfect white smile.

"Thank you," I say to her. Then I turn my attention to my daughter. "Zoey," I say softly. "Mama's going to sleep now. Are you sure you don't want to sleep in the bed with me?"

Zoey's eyes widen as though sleeping with me is a punishment. "Mommy, please! You promised I could have a living room sleepover with Lia and the dogs!"

I look at Lia, this young woman whom I hardly know, but who my daughter seems to think is her new best friend. "Lia…are you sure? You know it's okay to change your mind."

On the one hand, I am so desperate for a little help, I would love if she'd sleep in the living room with Zoey. The thought of a few hours alone, totally alone, in a strange bed, where no one and nothing can get to me… It sounds like heaven.

Morris is confident that Jerry hasn't followed us, and Leo has reassured me that as long as I don't have anything else electronic with me that Jerry could have installed any kind of software or app on, it is unlikely he has any idea where we are.

I can really, fully, finally breathe.

Lia curls onto her side and gives me a smile. "Pinkie-swear promise," she says. "Zoey and I are gonna leave the TV on quietly and watch shows until she falls asleep, even if that's at three in the morning. She's on spring break, and I'm on an adventure. This is awesome!"

"Thank you," I say. And I really am grateful. I kiss my little love goodnight and put a hand on Lia's arm. "I'll be right upstairs. If anything changes and you want to come upstairs, Leo promised the hall light will be on."

"All night," he says. Then he yawns and gives Lia a shy smile. "Goodnight, then. See y'all in the a.m. I showed Morris where everything is, so I'm turning in."

He heads down the hall, flicking on the lights so the path will be illuminated if the girls get up.

Clearly Zoey's infatuation for her new auntie Lia is even more powerful than her crush on Leo, because he is almost all the way up the stairs before she calls, "Goodnight, Leo!"

He looks back, ducking his head so he can see her from the top of the stairs. "'Night, Princess Zoey!"

I kiss Zoey one more time and remind her where the bathroom is if she needs to get up during the night. I repeat my promise to Lia, letting her know if she changes her mind and doesn't want to have a sleepover, she can send Zoey up or come and get me anytime.

"Come on, Mom." Morris rests a tattooed hand on my shoulder. "Let the kids have their fun."

I nod and follow him down the hall, watching my happy little girl until I'm too far away to see the living room.

When I reach the bedroom door, I hesitate and clutch my hands in front of my chest. "I think I'm going to sleep on the couch," I say and then turn back toward the living room. "I don't like the idea of leaving Zoey alone with a stranger."

"She's not alone with a stranger," Morris says. "Well, okay, she kind of is. But we're all right here. Nothing is going to happen to Zoey. I promise that."

"We don't know, Morris. I mean, anything...

Anything can happen at any time. You just never really know someone."

I clench my hands into fists. I know it isn't likely, but every horrifying possibility runs through my mind.

"Alice." Morris lowers his face to mine. "I've known Tiny a long time. And if he's been communicating with this girl for months, and he's brought her into his life, I trust her. Let's give trust a try until we have reason to doubt her."

I nod, not entirely convinced.

He has a point, though. I left my old life to start a new one.

And that means new people.

New friends.

New ways of doing everything.

"Okay," I say, louder this time.

"Fantastic," Morris says. "Now, are you going to let me tuck you into bed?"

The door that's closed is Leo's bedroom. There are two other rooms in the hallway. One is Leo's older brother's room. The brother has been gone for over a year, and Leo's cleaned the room up since his brother was last here, so Morris has volunteered to sleep there. That leaves the grandfather's former room for me.

I take a fast shower and get changed into sleep

shorts and a tank top before heading into the room where I'll be crashing tonight.

"Turndown service," Morris says, knocking lightly on the door.

I left the door ajar, so I smile and motion him inside. "What's involved in this turndown service?" I ask.

Morris hasn't changed or cleaned up yet. He's still wearing the jeans that fit his body like a second skin, but his boots are gone, and he's wearing only a plain white tank. He taps the bed.

"Climb in," he says.

I do and tuck in under the covers. I pat the bed beside me, inviting him to join me.

Morris climbs onto the bed, and I notice the mattress doesn't squeal under his weight. I scold myself for even thinking about quiet mattresses.

Morris sits beside me, and we lean against the simple wooden headboard.

"What a day, huh?" I ask, trying to make light of it.

Morris grabs one of my hands and laces his fingers through mine. "One for the books, that's for sure."

"What happens next?" I ask. "I keep running from Jerry. He finds me, I run again. How does this ever stop?"

Morris squeezes my hand. "Tomorrow, we get up.

We take it one hour at a time. We figure it out. And you don't run."

"Don't run?" I repeat. "Morris…" I shake my head and twist toward him in bed. "I've been running my whole life, and it hasn't made a bit of difference. I ran away from the grief when I lost my mom and ended up paying for that decision."

"You got Zoey out of the deal," he observes.

"Yes, but then look what I've given my daughter. A man to provide for us who'd rather see us scared and controlled than living the lives he provided for." I rest my head on Morris's shoulder, desperate for the comfort I know it will bring. I can't help thinking it may be the last time. Tomorrow, Jerry will find me, and this whole effort will have been for nothing.

Morris tilts his head closer to mine. I can smell the musk of his skin.

I close my eyes and drink it in for a moment. The heady fragrance of sunshine and sweat, oil and man.

He adjusts his legs on top of the blankets, and I sigh.

"What am I doing here? I have no job. I owe Leo a shit-ton of money for fixing my car. He's giving us a place to stay… I can never dig myself out of this hole. Maybe I should just go back to Jerry. Tell him he was right. I am a fucking cunt. A stupid, traitorous bitch who doesn't deserve the life he provides."

"He told you all that, did he?" Morris seems to take it all in stride, but he tightens his grip on my hand. "Well, let me tell you something, Alice Sparrow."

He traces the fingers of my left hand, the one interlaced with his, with his free hand. The light touch sends sparks trailing through my body, up my arm, through my chest. I can feel his presence beside me, and it's as if every ounce of my being is straining to get closer, to feel more of his touch.

"You ever hear of broken wings, little bird?" he asks.

I shake my head. "Is that a biker thing?"

He nods. "When a rider has a broken wings patch, it means that rider's been in a crash. Usually a pretty bad one."

I take a deep breath and focus on the richness of Morris's voice. His words vibrate through my body like he's speaking to my soul.

"But you don't just earn the patch by falling off the bike," he continues. "You earn the patch by getting back on. Riding again. Overcoming your fear and flying—even if you have broken wings."

I nod slightly. "Morris…" I know he's trying to make a point. "This isn't the same. I love what you're trying to do. It's sweet. You're so…sweet."

When I say that, Morris turns and grips me with a lightning-quick hand. He slides his fingers under my hair and twists so our faces are angled close.

"Baby," he says, his voice low and silky. "It's

exactly the same thing. You think we only fall once in life? We ride, we crash. We ride again, we crash again. Sometimes we're lucky, and we don't fall far enough or hard enough to do any permanent damage. But most of the time, a fall means bad news. Real bad. You're fucked up so bad, you're not sure you're gonna make it. But if you wanna earn that patch and ride again, you get back up. You ride again, Alice Sparrow."

Before I can form another argument, Morris sweeps his lips over mine.

"Morris," I gasp his name against his mouth.

In a flash, he's out of bed, and he's twisting the lock on the bedroom doorknob.

"Yes?" he asks, his eyes searing their heat into my skin.

My nipples pebble under my sleep tank at the question. I know what he is asking, and there's only one answer.

Yes.

Yes.

Yes.

Even if it's only for one night, even if it's the worst mistake I've made yet, I say it. I get back up on the ride. "Yes," I breathe.

Morris strips off his jeans, and I'm not at all surprised he's not wearing anything beneath them. I am ravenous as he strips off his tank, all muscles and arms and abs and hips.

I watch him, soaking in every ounce of his beauty, every inch of his strength.

He is massive and solid and…colorful. Tattoos cover his chest and arms, his back, even his hands and the sides of his neck. I could spend hours just tracing the shadows and shapes, memorizing them, asking for their stories.

But he gives me an even bigger distraction as my eyes travel down past his waist. Morris is hard as a rock, his cock thick.

I can't pull my eyes from his length as he crosses the bedroom in long, quick steps.

"Left on the light. Figured you liked what you saw," he says, smirking at me. "I know I'm gonna like what I see." He lifts his chin toward me. "Your turn. Get up."

"Up?"

We're both already in bed.

"I want the show, darlin'. I've been watching that ass bend, walk, and bounce all day. Now, get over there and show me what you got."

I curl my lips together in an embarrassed pucker. "You've been watching me all day?"

"Since the gas station," he says. "Now, get up. Go!"

He swats at me playfully, so I climb out of bed.

God, it has been such a long time since sex was fun. Since it was something I wanted, not just something I had to get through.

I almost don't know what to do, but then I see the way he looks at me.

Morris leans back on the bed, completely naked. He's unapologetically watching, waiting for me.

He wants me.

Me.

A man I've known for such a short time and yet whom I feel impossibly bound to.

I quirk a brow at him and vow to get out of my head. But then it hits me. I'm married.

"Morris," I say, my confidence plummeting into my toes.

"Darlin'?" he asks. "I've got stamina, but I don't know if I can take much more chatting."

"I'm...married," I say. "I—"

"Fuck that fucker," Morris says dismissively. "Do you love him? Is he good to you? Is he the man whose bed you climb into every night? Whose name you scream when you touch yourself all alone?"

I shake my head in disgust. "None of that. It has never been like that. Not with him. Not with anyone," I admit.

"You plan on filing for divorce?" he presses.

"First fucking chance I get."

"That's all I need to know. Now strip, baby. Please."

Somehow, his reassurance and the hidden fantasy I've nurtured all day of Morris's chin scraping along the contours of my body bring me more strength than

I realized I had. I give him a saucy twirl, and he settles back against the headboard.

"I love it, baby. You're so fucking gorgeous, Alice."

I don't exactly know where to start, but it's not like I have much on to take off, so I start with what I think he wants.

I turn around and face the door, so my back is toward Morris. I grab the hem of my tank top and slowly pull it up, lifting it over my waist and torso, and then slowly wriggle my shoulders until the tiny piece of material is over my head. I twirl it like I imagine a stripper would, and Morris starts cracking up.

"Love the theatrics, baby," he says. "Now, get to the main event."

Still facing the bedroom door, I bend slightly and stick out my ass toward Morris, smiling to myself.

He growls in response, a hungry moan that rattles deep in his chest.

"Fuck," he hisses. "Your body, baby."

I assume that's a good thing, so I continue, not looking back at him and not saying a word for fear I'll break the mood and scare away what little guts I've summoned.

I hook my fingers in the waistband of my sleep shorts and slowly work them down over my hips. I bend from the waist, so as I remove them, I'm slowly leaning forward and giving him a full, face-level view of my ass.

"Oh my fucking…" Morris's words and breathing

are thick, slow. His lids are heavy. "Alice," he says worshipfully. "Come to me, baby."

I turn and face him.

He has scrambled out of bed and stands naked with me beside the bed. He turns me to face the bed and holds my naked back to his front.

"You are exquisite," he breathes against my hair. He reaches his hands around my middle and cups my breasts in his hands.

I drop my head back against his chest, my legs already weak from the perfect pressure of his callused hands on my skin.

He pinches my nipples lightly, tugging and twisting as I gasp in pleasure.

"Like that?"

"Love it," I pant.

As he works my nipples between his fingertips, I sway on weak knees. My core is lava, on fire with a liquid heat that rushes so quickly, the sensation stuns me. I'm nothing anymore, no words, no resistance. I'm not worried about the world outside or anything other than the delicious, torturous bliss flowing from his fingers through my nipples.

"Perfect," Morris sighs. "Your body is perfection, baby. Your ass, your pussy."

He moves his hands from my breasts, and in those seconds he's gone, I miss him. I yearn for it. I want to reach out and claw at his hands, putting them back where they belong.

Me.

On me.

But I don't have to wait long before those hands are exploring my ass, kneading my cheeks and spreading me wide.

"Morris," I gasp, not certain what he's going to do. But again, I should just trust him. He's spread me open, and I feel the cool air from the room for just a second before the heat of his tongue flicks against my pussy.

I fall forward against the mattress, my feet still supporting my weight on the floor. Morris has dropped to his knees. His hands keep my ass spread wide while his tongue licks deep into my pussy.

"Fuck, you taste good," he pants. "Alice. Can't wait."

As much as I want to explore all of him, every inch, every taste, right now, the longing I feel, the raw hunger, almost make me crazy, rabid. I've never felt like this before.

It's as if a blindfold covers my eyes and all I see is a lust haze, and behind it, Morris's hands, his tongue, his fingertips finding my clit and stroking it in firm circles until I'm close to exploding.

"Morris," I warn, my legs trembling.

"Give it to me," he demands. "Open."

He spreads my ass cheeks wider with his hands and leaves all the work of my pleasure to his tongue. I don't know how he can reach my clit, but his tongue flicks and sucks me until I can't hold back the scream in my throat. I climax in volcanic shakes, my knees shuddering until I collapse facedown against the bed.

"You good, baby?" he asks, standing behind me.

I'm lying facedown like a reverse snow angel, speechless and weak. "I'm great," I whisper, too exhausted to speak.

"Don't have condoms here," he mutters.

"Doesn't matter," I say. "I'm good, IUD. Clean."

"Same," he says. "Except the birth control part."

I giggle, and before I can catch my breath, he's behind me. I feel his hands on my waist and he tries to scoot me forward on the bed, but I tense immediately.

"Not facedown," I say in a rush, cold starting to seep into my body. "I don't wanna be facedown," I say, and I struggle against his weight to flip over.

But I don't have to struggle.

He releases my hips and grabs one of my hands.

"Even better," he says. "I wanna watch your face while I fuck you until you come again."

"I'm not going to—" But the words fade on my lips as Morris straddles my hips and eases his way inside.

He doesn't thrust hard or fast, but he enters me slowly, inch by agonizing inch. I can hardly control the pleasure. I squeeze my eyes shut and clench the blankets in my fists, because he's right. I am going to come again.

His deep thrusts hit just the right angle. He's

kneeling on the bed, and my knees are in his hands, my feet in the air, and I'm open, exposed.

This is raw, wanton.

It feels wild and untamed.

I've never felt anything like this before. But with Morris inside me, I'm not shy. I'm not insecure. I'm a greedy bitch, planting my hands on the insides of my thighs and opening my legs as wide as I can for him.

After a few slow thrusts, my body responds with a rhythm all its own. I work my hips and hold open my thighs, watching through my lashes as Morris closes his eyes, opens his mouth, and pants through his climax.

We collapse beside each other on the bed, sweaty and breathless. As the erotic haze starts to lift, I listen for the sounds in the house around us.

"I better clean up," I say. I slip my pajamas back on and leave Morris faceup, eyes closed, dick still hard on the bed.

I use the hallway bathroom, relieved to hear undisturbed chatter from Lia and Zoey coming from downstairs. I can hear Leo snoring through his closed bedroom door, so at least he wasn't disturbed by our quiet coupling. I clean up and dry myself off, and then I grab a fresh hand towel to bring to Morris.

When I get back to the bedroom, he's snoring lightly with an arm draped over his face. I smile at the sight and marvel at the fact that he's dozed off, and yet his cock is still semi-hard

I climb into bed beside him. I tug on the covers and roll onto my side.

"Mmm," he says. "Good, baby?"

It's a sleepy question, but it's also the answer. "Good, baby," I echo.

Then Morris surprises me by lifting his head and planting a featherlight kiss on my lips.

That soft touch, loving and tender, promises more. Promises more than just getting back up after a crash. Morris's kiss promises me that I *am* getting back up after the fall. I'm earning the patch. And as I fall asleep in Morris's arms, I have a glimmer of hope that maybe, just maybe, I've earned my broken wings.

CHAPTER
EIGHTEEN
MORRIS

WHEN I TURN over in the middle of the night, my dick finds Alice's ass cheeks and immediately wakes me up. I peer around the unfamiliar room, and it all comes back.

We're at Leo's house. A guy I didn't even know twenty-four hours ago. And now I'm under the covers with a woman who, likewise, was a stranger to me until yesterday morning.

But she's no longer a stranger.

She's sound asleep on her side, the curve of her ass nestled tightly against me. In the quiet, I can hear her breathing, soft and sweet against the hand she has tucked under her cheek. My eyes have adjusted to the dark, and I see a digital clock on the dresser.

Two a.m.

I wonder, if I wake her up, if she's the kind of

woman who'll swat me away and try to crawl back into her dreams. I suspect Alice is the other kind.

The best kind of woman.

My dick won't let me rest until I find out what kind of woman Alice is.

I tuck in a little closer to her, and my erection nudges her cheeks through her pajamas. I stroke her hair, brushing it back from her face, and I'm gifted with a whiff of that spun-sugar fragrance. How Alice smells like candy even when she's sound asleep, I don't know, but I don't question it. Because as I touch her, she stirs slightly under the covers.

At first, she huffs a little sleep-heavy sigh, but soon, her hips press back against me.

"Mmm," she mumbles, and I can't tell if she's awake or not, but the sounds she's making seem to suggest she's trying to drag herself back into consciousness.

I take this as the invitation I want, and I slip a hand under the waistband of her shorts. I don't do anything more than palm her ass cheek, but the heat of my hand on her skin seems to jolt her awake. She stretches her body, and I can just picture her toes curling as her feet meet mine under the sheets.

"Mmm…Morris," she whispers. "What time is it?"

"Middle of the night, baby," I answer, kneading and massaging her firm cheeks in my hands.

"Oh God," she sighs, "Morris…"

If I had any doubt before, I now know what kind of woman my baby is. Alice reaches for her waistband and tugs her pajama shorts down around her ankles before kicking them off. She reaches a hand behind her and touches my cock, which is jutting dangerously close to her ass. She pulls her fingers away from my body just long enough to slip them into her mouth. What seems like a second later, she's stroking the underside of my cock, wetting it with the saliva on her fingertips.

"Fuck," I croak. It's like her fingers already know my body, already know just the ridges and veins to touch, the right pressure and the right speed. "Alice…"

I want her again.

I want her in every way.

In the light, so I can watch her.

In the dark, so I can conjure the memory of her sinfully stunning face as I bring her to the brink and back.

I want this—this woman, this feeling every night. In my bed, in my life. Even as she encircles my cock with her entire hand and strokes me, feeling every inch from the jutting base to the weeping tip, I know she's got a kid, a shitty ex who wants her back or worse, and a whole lifetime of problems I'm probably better off without.

But then I think of the caramel in her eyes. Those

perfect nipples, thick and tender between my fingertips.

The way she smiles and tickles her daughter. How she braids hair and washes dishes. And I think there's no lifetime of problems I wouldn't face if it means I get to have this.

Come home to this.

To her.

To Alice.

"Baby," I pant. "I wanna see you."

"No," she murmurs. "Don't get up. Don't wanna wait."

She rolls over onto her side and faces me, then awkwardly shrugs out of her tank top and tosses it on the floor. "That was my second sexiest move," she teases.

I grin at that.

My sweet little bird.

Funny, sexy, broken little bird. But, no. She's not broken.

She's just learning to fly again.

We try to make out each other's faces in the dark. The windows let in a little moonlight, and I can see the sparkle of her bright teeth when she smiles. The purse of her lips when I reach between us and stroke her breasts.

Earlier, I needed her fast. I needed her every way, but I couldn't make any of it last long enough. Never would I get my fill of this woman.

Of her body, her sweetness.

Her natural sugar.

I trace my fingers around her nipples, erect and tender under my touch. I can tell how much she likes it, how much that turns her on. She flutters her eyes closed and pants my name.

"More?" I ask. "Harder or…?"

"Harder," she gasps. "But not too hard."

I hold back a laugh, loving that she trusts me enough to tell me what she wants, and trusts me enough to test the boundaries that I can only discover by trying.

I twist that erect peak a little between my thumb and index finger, then release it to a disappointed-sounding whoosh of air from her lips. I don't make her wait long for my touch, but I alternate the pressure, teasing my fingertips lightly over her skin before pinching her again with my fingers.

"Oh God!" she cries, arching her back and jutting her tits toward me.

"Good," I whisper. "I wanna hear you moan, baby."

"No moaning," she pants. "People…kids…"

"Shh." I hush her worries. She can moan out if she wants. She can stifle her pleasure if that makes her feel more comfortable.

What I want right now is all of her.

I want to feel her juices on my cock, taste her on my fingers.

I want to claim her body with mine while I feast on her mouth.

I want Alice Sparrow, and my hunger for her seems insatiable.

"On top," she whispers and starts to scramble out from under the sheets.

"Yeah. Fuck yeah," I say. I lie on my back and search for her face in the darkness, but what I feel instead is her mouth, warm and wet, as she takes my cock deep.

Ohhhhh fuck.

That's my baby.

That's my Alice.

She's working her tongue on the underside of my dick, just below the head. Her soft mouth on that tender little nook makes me want to blow right there on her face, but I can't. Won't.

I need inside. Inside her mouth, inside her hot, perfect pussy.

She grips my dick in her hand and seems to take her sweet time, licking the shaft, kissing and dragging her teeth ever so lightly along my length. She palms my balls and cups them in her hand, stroking two fingertips between the base of my sac and my ass, nearly sending me through the roof.

"Fuck," I sputter and reach for her.

If I don't stop feeling her, if I let myself go any further, I won't be able to come back.

She moves away from my dick but only long

enough to straddle my hips. When she lifts her bare leg and the moonlight reflects off her skin, it takes everything I have not to grab her and pull her down onto my dick. But I want to learn what she wants from me. She needs this control. She needs to guide her weight over my body.

I watch pleasure move across her face as she lowers herself onto my erection.

Unlike earlier, Alice nearly slams onto my body and then just sinks down on me, lowering her head and opening her lust-dusky eyes.

"You feel… You're so…"

I know what she's trying to say, but words escape me too. I fill her. I can feel the way her walls stretch, the way she clenches lightly around me as if her body wants to draw me as far in as I can go.

She steadies her breathing and then starts to rock against me, gentle, slow strokes at first, finding the rhythm. Her tits are bouncing with every grind of her hips, her hard nipples teasing me, begging for my touch.

I don't want to move, don't want to shift and ruin the pace she's setting. I can tell by the intensity of her movements, she's getting lost, losing herself in the pure pleasure of my cock stroking the places no one else can reach. Her thighs tremble and strain with the effort, and I hold those legs with my hands, wanting to feel that velvet skin, her smooth, strong body working over mine.

"Morris," she pants, and she opens her eyes in a rush, looking dazed.

"Come for me," I whisper softly, "God, Alice, I want you so much."

I reach up and twist her nipples, and with a small, muffled cry, Alice trembles on my dick. Her body vibrates, shuddering and shaking.

We climax together, Alice finishing first but not moving until she's sure every last wave of my orgasm has slowed to a stop.

We don't move for a few heated moments. My legs are trashed, tense and tight from holding her weight, working against her movements in a way I didn't even realize I was. She opens her eyes slowly, squinting at me as though she needs to use every ounce of strength she has left to open her eyes.

She lifts herself off me and practically crawls back under the covers beside me.

"Baby," she croons. "Morris?"

"Hmm-mm," I say, already on my side, ready to tuck her back against me.

"You're amazing," she whispers. "That was amazing."

"First of many amazing times," I say. "Thousands. Probably millions. At least, until we get our own place. After that, I'll lose count."

She giggles and works her way backward so our bodies are spooned together tight as can be. And we fall back asleep to finish out this first of many amazing nights to come.

———————

I wake in the morning to Alice leaning over me, kissing me goodbye. The sunlight is streaming weakly into the bedroom, and based on how fresh Alice smells, she's already showered.

When I open my eyes, I can see she's dressed. "Time?" I mumble.

Alice strokes my face scratching her nails against the scruff of my beard. "Early," she says. "But I want to make sure I'm up before Zoey."

I nod, figuring some kind of internal mom clock must have awakened her. After the night we had, I can't imagine waking up for anything other than another round.

"Lots to do today," she says sweetly. "I'll see you when you get up."

"Alice…" I reach for her and grab her hand.

She sits down beside me on the bed, and I scoot over to give her more room.

"Don't," she says, but there is a smile in her words. "Don't you dare tempt me back in that bed, or I may never get out."

I kiss the back of her hand and shove the sheets aside. I look down at all the parts of me that want to wish Alice a good morning. "I'm all about temptation, sweetheart. You oughta know that by now."

She stares at my cock, no doubt reconsidering this whole getting-up-early thing. But then she shakes her head. "I don't know when we'll be able to…" She trails off, looking wistful. "Zoey may want to sleep with me tonight. Lia may want her own room. Maybe you'll end up back at the compound or at your place…"

I pull her close and wrap a hand behind her neck. Her hair is damp from the shower, and it smells like a cocktail a girl like Lia would drink on vacation. Fruity, sweet, and totally free. "My place is where you are," I say. "From now on."

"Morris…you don't have to say that." Alice shakes her head. "Today's when things get real. I'm going to have to face—"

"We," I correct. "*We*'re going to have to face a whole day when we can't just be naked and bouncing on Leo's old man's bed."

Alice laughs. "Well, when you put it that way…"

I give her a kiss on the forehead. "I'm going to get the electricity turned back on at the building, first thing. Leo can get started on repairing that car. Zoey's going to need a school, and figuring out where you're going to stay will determine where we can get her into school."

"I need a job," Alice adds. "And a phone." She sighed. "So much to do."

"One thing at a time," I remind her.

Something in her eyes darkens then. She's spiraling. Pulling away from the heat and warmth and bubble of our night together as she thinks about the work ahead. The strength it takes to start over. To pick yourself up and keep going.

"Alice," I remind her. "It's not just you against the world anymore. Me, you, a girl crew. A couple bikers and a love-sick mechanic. What could go wrong with a family like that?"

At the word family, she lowers her head. Looks down at her bare feet. She nods, but it's the most unconvincing, uncertain gesture.

It's as if I can physically feel the walls rolling back up to protect her, shutting me out. Shutting out everything that's been building between us.

"Family," she repeats, trying the word on in slow, tentative syllables.

"What this is, whatever it becomes, it's real," I tell her. "Last night wasn't just about a piece of ass. It wasn't for me, and I know it wasn't for you either."

She flushes, and a tiny smile picks up the corners of her lips. "It was amazing. Last night was…"

"It was. And it will be. Tonight and as many nights as I can reasonably have you. Now, get," I say, kissing her once on the lips. "Before I decide I want you again five times before breakfast."

Alice casts a quick look down at my dick, which continues to remind her he's really happy to see her this morning. She smiles and nods, giving my thigh a playful squeeze, then leaves the bedroom and closes the door behind her. The caramel in her eyes looks cold as she walks away.

If I want to keep this little bird from falling again, I'm going to have to work fast.

CHAPTER
NINETEEN
ALICE

I TIPTOE down the hallway with a smile on my face for the first time in years. My nipples feel bruised but in the best possible way. Every time I move, the friction of my clothes against my skin pulls me back into the memories of last night.

Morris's touch, the sounds he made.

He opened something inside me I didn't realize I had.

Morris is a skilled lover, but it was more than him knowing what to do. He wanted to learn, to explore every inch of my most private places and discover their secrets. How much pressure on my tits made me wet. How hard to move, how fast. I've never been with anyone like him.

I only wish it could last.

But I'm no fool.

He is gorgeous, single, and a biker.

He's not family material. And definitely not looking to tie himself down to someone like me, with tons of baggage.

The thought that, in a few days, I'll be alone brings a chill up the back of my spine. I'll have to find my way, and that's okay.

I'll do it.

I'll provide for my daughter and pay back all my debts to Morris and Leo.

There is no other way it can be.

When I reach the living room, I can see that Lia is wide awake. She's sitting up in the nest of blankets on the floor, her back propped against the couch. She's got the two little dogs, one under each arm, and her cell phone in her hands. The bigger dog lifts its head when it sees me, but a quick shushing sound from Lia, and it lays its head back down.

"Good morning," I whisper, giving the girl a big smile. "How did you sleep?"

Zoey is passed out cold beside Lia, her face poking out from beneath the corner of a teal quilt.

Lia nods happily. She gives me a thumbs-up and sets the puppies down. She shushes the dogs again and then quietly climbs through the blanket fort to join me in the kitchen. The dogs trot after her, panting and clicking their nails on the tile floor.

Lia peeks out the kitchen door into the backyard, and then she unlocks the deadbolt and lets the dogs out to do their business.

"They're okay out there by themselves?" I ask, keeping my voice low so I won't wake Zoey. "They won't run off?"

Lia shakes her head. "They've run off in the past. You know, if, like, a bunny or something really exciting caught their eye. But we lived for a year in my van, and all that time, I only had one leash. They learned to stay close to me if they wanted a warm bed and food."

I look the girl over and risk asking the question on my mind. "Why were you living in your van? If you don't mind my asking?" I sort through Leo's kitchen for the coffee and filters.

Lia stares out over the yard, watching her pets. "I don't mind at all." She opens the door a crack and whistles, and all three dogs come running. She holds up a finger, and all three sit patiently, waiting to be let in. "Remind me later to clean up Leo's yard," she says.

I nod and laugh and brew the max amount of coffee Leo's coffeemaker can produce. I head to the fridge and pull out some items to throw together a small breakfast.

There's not much here, so shopping, if we end up staying, will be high on the list of things to do.

As much as I could live half the day on coffee, and the rest of the adults probably could too, Zoey will need to eat and keep a regular schedule as much as possible.

"So, the van story," Lia says. "It was just one of those things, you know? After high school, Mom really wanted me to go to college. To pick a career, to get on the path." Lia shrugs. "I couldn't imagine anything worse than another four years like the ones I'd spent in high school. Hours locked behind a desk, doing things other people said were important. So, I took off," she says. "We were living in Tennessee at the time, so if you can imagine lots of farmland, wide-open spaces. I used the graduation money from my grandparents to buy a van, and me and all three of the pups set out for parts unknown."

"You were eighteen?" I ask. I can't imagine. "Did you have a plan?"

Lia shakes her head. "No plan what I would do, where I would go. I only knew I wanted to get away from all the stuff I didn't want. School, a job. A nine-to-five, I guess I should say."

"Coffee?" I ask, pouring myself a mug and setting out a second for her.

She nods. "Thanks."

I put sugar and milk on the table before I sit across from her. "So, where did you go? Were you terrified? Excited?"

"Yes. All of it. All of the feelings."

"I'm so practical," I explain. "Maybe it's from being a mom, but I can't imagine how you slept, where you went to the bathroom…"

The pretty young woman across from me laughs

and shakes her head. "You know the number one thing I learned in my time on the road? That it all just comes. Good comes, bad comes. I couldn't stop any of it. Couldn't prepare for it."

I hear the sound of the shower turning off upstairs. Morris or Leo must be awake.

"So, that's it," she says. "Hard shit happened. Weather and flat tires. Running out of money or food. Finding myself in spots I didn't think I'd be able to get out of. But somehow, every single day, I woke up alive and ready to meet the adventure as it came. I found places to eat and sleep. I met people along the way. I took a ton of pictures and saw the country the way I wanted to."

"But you found your way here?" I ask.

I'm still not convinced that adventure sounds like fun.

"Yeah." She nods thoughtfully. "I did."

I feel like she has more to say, but she sips her coffee and doesn't seem in any rush to get there.

"Alice, may I speak freely?"

The formality of the question surprises me. "Uh, sure," I say.

She looks me over and reaches across the table. "I thought I was choosing something that was just for me, you know? The freedom to wake up under the sunrise and sleep under the stars if I chose to. I listened to what I wanted on the radio. I sang at the top of my lungs. I ate at hole-in-the-wall places and let my dogs run free in random fields. It was a great time, but when I closed my eyes at night, I always felt like I was hiding from something. I was lying to myself, even while I was telling myself I was choosing the path less traveled. Running away from what I didn't want for my life didn't create the life I wanted. For me, there was a big difference between taking a chance and making a choice."

I tilt my head, not entirely sure where she's going with all this. "Which was leaving? The choice or the chance?"

"The choice," she says without hesitation. "Because while every day was a mystery and nothing was certain, I also had…nothing. I was free, and that felt different than I thought staying home and being confined to an office or a classroom would. But the real test was taking a chance on making the kind of life I wanted."

Her face grows less animated, thoughtful as she talks about her mom.

"You know, my mom wanted me to work in sales. She said with my personality, my looks, I'd make a ton of money and do really well in sales if I didn't want to go to college. And maybe she was right. I mean…" She shrugs.

"So, you came here?" I prod. I'm not sure there's a lesson in this story, but I'm willing to wait for it.

"I did," she confirms. "I've done it all. Well, not everything. I never did go to work at the car rental place, and I've never worked in sales. Not in the way my mom meant for me to. I've been a dog walker and groomer, a nanny. I've house-sat for people, taken care of old folks. Cut lawns." She shrugs. "But I never lost the lessons I learned on the road."

She meets my eyes. "It all just comes, Alice. We can't prepare for it. We can't stop most of it. Sometimes we can run from it, but we can't *out*run it. You always have a choice. How you want to live. Who you want to be. Who you want to let in. I think I decided I'd rather face it my way than spend my time looking at life in a rearview mirror."

I consider that. Consider the hippie wisdom of this young woman and wonder whether that's what I'm doing. Facing my life or running from it.

"I always knew I had a dad out there," she says. "And I have a little secret," she admits. "I always knew his name. I always knew how to find him."

"What?" I can't believe she's trusting me with this.

She nods. "Finding my dad was what I was really running from. I realized that after a while. I used to be mad at him because he never knew me, never tried. But I realized my mom probably knew, deep down, that a twenty-year-old biker she'd met in a bar probably wouldn't have been a good dad, and she never told him. And Tiny's cool and all, but Mom knew he wasn't her soul mate. But he was my dad. And in my mind, I understood that until I found him and knew him, until I knew about that missing half of who I am, I would never really know what I wanted from life. I would have just driven aimlessly, always wishing I'd pointed my van in the direction of my dad. Until, finally, I did it."

Things are starting to make sense to me.

"Everything comes," she says. "But our truth won't find us until we're ready to face it."

"You're very wise for your age, Lia."

"Thank you." She smiles, pushing the coffee mug to the side. "I'm going to see if I can get a turn in that shower. Then I'm going to make breakfast smoothies." She blows noisy kisses to her dogs and rinses her mug in the sink. Then she trots over to me and gives me a sweet smile. "I'm glad I landed with you guys. Zoey's like the little sister I always wanted and never had."

She plods through the living room and checks on Zoey as she passes. She turns back and holds her hands in a prayer pose on the side of her face.

I smile my thanks and refill my coffee.

She's a sweet girl. Kind, independent. I'm glad she's landed with us as well. I think about what she said. What would I do if I had the freedom to choose anything? I think about my life coming for me, happening whether I plan for it, whether I build it, or whether I stand on the horizon and watch, waiting for it to reach me.

Does that life include Morris?

Is he what's meant for me?

Or is he just a distraction in the rearview while I'm running from Jerry?

I don't know what I believe anymore.

I've got the wisdom of a biker, a hippie girl, and the demands of a husband steering me every which way. I think that's the problem.

I'm surrounded by people who know what they want. Who know who they are and their place in their world. I'm still finding my way. Battered between a life I didn't make but chose with Jerry on the one hand, and the vast, terrifying unknown of making something from literally nothing on the other.

In truth, I've got a beater car that's dead on blocks. I have a daughter who won't be able to drink herbal smoothies with the dogs for breakfast. I need to find a job, a home, and that nine-to-five life if I don't want everything to fall apart. I appreciate what Lia said, and I'm glad she's found her father.

But I don't know if I've ever felt more lost, torn between choices and chances.

CHAPTER
TWENTY
MORRIS

"IT'S RATED PG, ZOEY," Alice says. Her back is to the table as she cleans the coffeemaker over the sink. Just seeing her from behind makes my dick jump in appreciation and recognition of last night. I shove away thoughts of our middle-of-the-night romp and focus on the work ahead.

"PG?" Leo seems to pout with Zoey. "Come on, Alice. She may only be… Wait, Zoey, how old are you?"

"I'm six," she says, sipping a glass of water. "But I'm an incredibly mature six."

Somehow, I bite back my laughter at her response, but part of me is sad for the little girl. She shouldn't be so mature for her age, but I know it's because of her stepfather.

Leo nods. "She totally is, Alice. I mean, I could watch this dragon show with her, and you know, maybe Lia too. And if it's scary, well, she'll have two grown-ups right there, and we can change it."

"Oh my God, Mom, please?" Zoey sounds far older than her six years, and Alice whirls with a scolding look on her face.

"Zoey," she says with a sigh. "I don't know." Alice catches a glimpse of me coming into the kitchen, and her demeanor immediately changes.

"Come on, Mom," I whine, joining in the fun. "I mean, Oh. My. God. It's a dragon."

Leo starts cracking up as I imitate a teenage girl's voice. Zoey shocks me by leaping up from her chair and running up to me. She hesitates when she reaches my legs but then grins up at me.

"'Morning, princess," I say, patting her head.

She gives me a fast, light hug, her arms circling my legs because she's so tiny. She even closes her eyes for a second as if she's really giving herself over to the hug.

And goddamn, if there was anything hard left in my heart, it all melted into a puddle looking into her sweet caramel eyes. Damn kids.

"Good morning, Morris. I'm so glad you're up. Mommy really does not understand how mature I am." Zoey whirls on a surprisingly glittery sock and plunks back into her chair. "Don't you think I should be able to watch it?"

My gaze swings to Alice.

"Finish your fruit," Alice says to Zoey, giving me a smile.

I clap Leo on the shoulder and wish him a good morning, then meet Alice at the sink and plant a kiss on her lips right in front of everyone.

"Oh my God, Mom…" Zoey says. She covers her mouth with her hands and starts giggling hysterically.

I can see how impressionable kids are. One night around new people and she's picked up all these grown-up phrases from Lia.

"Zoey," Alice says, that mom tone on full blast again. "Why don't you go brush your teeth and find your shoes? We have things to do today."

Lia shoves open the kitchen door and walks toward the sink. "Leo, the yard is all cleaned up after the dogs, but you should know what's in your trash bin."

"That's okay," he says a little too quickly. "You didn't have to do that."

It seems I'm not the only love-sick puppy in this house.

Lia washes her hands at the sink and plops down beside Leo. She helps herself to a slice of toast from his plate and looks from me to Alice.

"So, what's the plan for the day?" she asks. "I was kind of hoping I could take Zoey and buy some arts and crafts. She's never made origami banners, and I was thinking, if it's all right with you, Leo, we could get some fairy lights and some patterned paper and really start to dress up that backyard."

Leo's eyes are like saucers. I can almost hear the wheels in his head—and heart—spinning. "Dress up the backyard. Uh, yeah… That sounds, uh, great."

That woman could have told him she was planning to barbecue one of her dogs in the backyard, and he probably would have asked for light relish and handed her a bag of charcoal. He's totally gone for her.

I look at Alice and then to Leo. "I called the power company. There's an outstanding balance both on the electric and the gas service that somehow wasn't cleared when the sale went through. I need to hit the compound and grab the paperwork from the closing and then head to the power company's office to sort this out. Second stop is the electricity service center. They told me they will turn on the power with proof of the property transfer, but that we'll need to sort out the bills through the club attorney I used for the closing."

"So, how fast do you think they'll get the power on?" Leo asks. "I can start working as soon as the building has juice."

"They told me immediately, so you'll have power today. How would you feel about heading to the building and waiting for me there? You can let me know when the power's on."

Leo nods. "Sounds good. What else?"

"We need to get Alice a phone. I can't be without mine, and we need to be able to reach each other."

"I have like, three," Lia says.

"What? You have three phones?" Leo looks at her like she said she cured cancer last summer and just decided to casually announce it over buttered toast.

She finishes a scrap of crust from Leo's plate and nods. "Yep. I use one, but I have Mom's and the one I had before this one. I never made it back to the store to return them. Kinda thought maybe I'd donate them. But yeah, that never happened." She shrugs. "You can have it. That way, you won't have to buy the device."

"Thank you, Lia." Alice looks near tears. "Let me pay for it."

"You're giving me a place to stay," Lia says. "I mean Leo is, but y'all have this motley crew family thing going on, so…no biggie."

Alice looks relieved.

We decide how to split up the most critical issues for the day. Leo will cover the shop and the building, waiting for the power to go on. I'll hit the compound for the paperwork and then will get the utilities turned back on. Lia will ride with me to the compound and will pick up her van from where she left it parked by Tiny's bike.

"We need to shop," Alice tells me. "Groceries. Dog food."

I nod. "Okay, why don't you come with me so you

can manage the shopping part. Lia, Leo, give Alice a list of whatever you want. Beer, wine, snacks. We'll get enough stuff to get us through the next couple of days, so don't be shy."

"Zoey comes with us, right?" Alice asks.

I nod. "Whatever you want."

Lia looks disappointed. "Okay, but you have to let me get crafts and stuff. I sort of promised a themed sleepover tonight. Art party and facials. Is Zoey too young to use a sheet mask?"

I shrug because I really have no clue what a sheet mask is, but Alice shakes her head, letting me know she has it under control.

"No. She's not too young," Alice answers.

"One last question…" Lia says. "The dogs."

"What about them?" I ask.

"They are pretty used to being with me all day, every day," Lia says.

"Why don't you bring them to the shop?" Leo suggests. "I can open up one of the empty storefronts, and you and the dogs and Zoey can come too and play in there once the power is back on."

"I don't know if puppies and a kid at the shop is such a good idea. I haven't even been inside yet, and I don't know if there's anything unsafe." I look to Alice. "I think we should probably keep Zoey with us today."

Leo shakes his head. "I do, and I have those keys for you, Morris. All the storefronts are pretty well cleaned out. Counters and light fixtures, but it's actually pretty ideal for dogs and kids. Nothing to hurt or to get hurt on."

Alice surprises me by smiling at Lia. "You know, I think we should let Zoey choose." She looks at me. "If Lia is okay taking Zoey for the day, they can turn on the phone and then go to the craft store and meet us at your building for lunch. We'll pick up the phone and Zoey, and we can either figure out what else needs to be done, or we can come back here and start cleaning, cooking. If we're going to be staying here for a while, I'd like to get a system down so Leo doesn't mind the houseguests."

"I don't mind," Leo says, staring straight at Lia. "I don't mind at all."

"Does that work for you, Lia? We can all ride together to the compound to get your van, and then we'll let Zoey choose if she wants to go with you and the pups or me and Morris." Alice seems to have forged some new connection to Tiny's daughter.

I like it.

I like what that means a lot.

"I should call my sister today," Alice says quietly as we climb out of the truck. "Once we have the new phone."

"You wanna check in now?" I ask, handing her

my phone. While Lia tumbles out of the back with the dogs, I tell Alice the passcode to unlock the device. She looks at me like I just whipped out my dick in broad daylight in the middle of an elementary school playground. "What?" I ask.

"Morris, you don't have to tell me your passcode." She's holding my phone like she expects a bunch of dick pics and pussy shots from other women to jump from the screen.

"No secrets between us, baby," I say. I slide off my sunglasses and clip them to the inside of my T-shirt. "I trust you completely."

She just watches me as I climb out of the car. "You've got my phone," I toss at her. "Take a picture, it'll last longer." I give her a smirk, and she flushes.

"Morris," she asks, sounding a little hesitant. She's helping Zoey out of the booster seat and onto the paved parking pad. "Can Zoey and I come inside?"

I resist the urge to slap my knee and break out into laughter. "Yeah," I tell her. "You can all come inside. You'd be surprised how tame a club compound is during the day." I lean close and whisper in Alice's ear. "Just let me get a head start so I can clear out the coke and the strippers."

She gives me a horrified look, and I let a laugh rip.

"Adorable," I say, shaking my head. "Come on in."

We head inside, and, of course, the first person we

see is Midge. She gives Lia a wave but makes a beeline for Alice and me. She peers at us and then at Zoey.

"Lots of changes around here," Midge quips. "Woulda been nice if someone told me the club was opening a day care."

"Real funny," I say, not at all amused. "This here's my girl, Alice," I say, nodding, "and her daughter, Zoey. I assume you already met Lia."

Midge sniffs and lifts her chin at us, clearly none too pleased to have the estrogen bus pulling up to the compound and letting off a whole load of female talent.

Midge has the face of a walnut and the body of a melted candle, so three stunners like Alice, Zoey, and Lia are bound to ruffle the old gal's feathers.

"You'll always be our number one, Midge," I say, then give her a saucy smack on the ass behind the kitchen counter where Zoey won't notice.

Alice clearly does, her eyes widening, but I give her a wink and figure I'll explain later.

"Do you have any juice?" Zoey asks Midge, walking up to the counter. "Is this your kitchen? It's really pretty." She runs a finger along a barstool perched nearby. "Can I sit on this?"

Midge looks like she's about to blow a gasket, but then she shocks me by giving Zoey a full-mouth smile.

I'm shocked again as I look and see how few teeth old Midge really has. I don't think I've ever seen her smile, definitely not one of these full-gum reveals.

"Do you like orange juice?" Midge asks. "I happen to have some ice-cold orange juice right here."

Zoey and Midge set to work on finding juice, and Lia goes on the hunt to find her father.

I grab Alice's hand and lead her to my room. The door is closed, and there's a placard on the door with my name and position engraved on it.

"You're the vice president of the club?" she asks.

I nod. "It's part of the reason why I don't spend much time at that apartment. I stay here, close to my brothers. Close to the business."

She follows me into my room, and when we're safely inside, I close the door and whirl Alice around, pressing her backside against the closed door.

"How much time do you think we have?" I ask, nudging her legs open with a knee. I lower my face to her neck and just breathe her in. "Alice," I grit out, my dick dancing against my denim.

"I think you should find your paperwork, and I should call my sister," Alice says, but her actions don't fit her words.

She's pressed the flat of her hand against my hard cock and is rubbing firm circles over my dick.

"Jesus, baby." I press myself against her and work my hips in slow, torturous movements, grinding against her.

"Oh, Morris. No, no, no...we can't." She's grinning like a greedy teenager in the back seat of a car, telling me no with her words and yes with her body, her eyes, and that wicked smile. "I mean, yes, we will, but not now."

"Ahhh, fuck it." I cough and shake my head to clear the cobwebs and push away from my girl. "Tonight," I say. "Don't expect to get any sleep."

"RAYNE HASN'T HEARD another word from Jerry." Morris and I are heading back to the kitchen to grab Zoey from where we left her sipping juice with Midge.

"Yeah?" Morris asks. "Maybe the asshole figured he's been outmaneuvered. You left him, and he's going to go home and eat crow."

"I don't think so," Alice says quietly. "He's probably working out his next move. I told my sister we'll be getting a new number, so to wait to hear from us next."

"You just missed Lia," Midge says as we round the corner and head into the kitchen. "She's out moving Zoey's booster seat into her van."

Tiny lumbers into the kitchen and yanks open the fridge. "Whoa," he says, looking from Alice to Zoey and then back at me. "Last thing I expected to see here this morning." He grabs two cans of Coke and cracks them both open.

"Tiny, are you going to drink both of those? For breakfast?" Zoey's eyes are wide.

Tiny looks down at the cans in his hands like he's been caught stealing. "Uh, no. No. Here, Midge." He sets a can down in front of her.

"I don't drink that crap, and you know it." Midge scowls, but then she looks at Zoey and rolls her eyes. "They were both for him," she says, ratting him out.

"I know," Zoey says and giggles.

"Dad, I'm glad you're up." Lia comes running into the kitchen, all three dogs trotting at her heels. "I don't think I'm going to be able to use my van to run errands today. Zoey's booster is too wide to fit on the vintage seat. Can I borrow yours? I'll leave you my van keys if you want them."

Tiny shakes his head. "Nah, kid, I'm good. Take my truck. Whatcha doin' today?"

"We're going to the craft store!" Zoey practically shrieks.

Tiny flinches at the high pitch of her voice, but he recovers and nods. "All right, all right. Yeah."

He heads out to help Lia get the booster seat moved into his truck, muttering about dog hair on his seats. I can hear Lia's twinkly laugh as she promises to clean up after them.

She's a good egg. A good kid. I'm happy at the idea of her spending the day with Zoey.

They won't be far, and Morris has her number. She's promised to check in every hour, and we'll be meeting up at the building by lunchtime.

This will be good for Zoey. Good for all of us.

As we split up and head out to tackle the day's to-do list, I can almost start to breathe freely.

Morris is at my side. My daughter is with friends. We have a plan and work to do. I can almost imagine this feeling, this sense of lightness and freedom in my belly, is what hope feels like.

I learn a lot about Morris by the way he handles his business at the utility companies. The long lines, the completely disengaged employees, and the simmering morning heat have me frazzled and crabby, but Morris seems to take every moment in stride. He sweet-talks the grumpy old lady in line in front of us, who seems to have no concept of what it means to use an "inside voice."

When it's our turn at the counter, and the gas company employee tells Morris something completely opposite from what he was told on the phone this morning, he doesn't lose his cool. Doesn't threaten, doesn't pound his fists.

He respectfully explains what he heard and walks the grizzled man behind the counter step by step through what he thinks he should do.

I watch him as he talks, the way he uses his body to disarm people. He's a huge man and the tattoos, beard, and boots make him appear imposing, but I notice when he's talking to the morbidly obese man behind the counter, he lowers himself and leans on the counter so he's meeting the man at eye level.

He's never unkind.

Never loses his cool.

Morris is a true gentleman.

By the time we finish, we've gotten texts from Leo confirming that we have electricity at the building. The gas will take a little longer, but we have every assurance from Thad, Morris's new best friend at the customer service counter, that the gas will be back on before the end of the day.

We climb into his truck at the end of a productive morning. I slide my sunglasses over my eyes, and Morris reaches across the center console for my hand. We don't talk, but we make the ride from Daytona back to the shop with the lull of the road noise for company. Morris is quiet as we're driving and seems a little distracted. Maybe preoccupied with the work ahead.

It's funny how foreign this thing between us feels. How close we can be under the sheets or at the dinner table, but every new thing we do together reveals a fresh layer of him to understand. To interpret.

"Everything okay?" I ask.

He flicks a glance to the rearview mirror and then back at me. "Absolutely. You?"

"Mmm." And it's true. I am okay. Better than okay, actually.

My mind wanders to Jerry. How different this morning would have been if he'd been the one dealing with the utilities. Jerry only knows how to communicate through manipulation and force. Coercion and belittling. And when none of that works, threats.

"You were amazing today," I say, squeezing Morris's hand.

Morris flicks me a confused look. "Hmm? Just getting shit done, sweetheart."

I shake my head. "No, really. You were so patient and respectful. Even when everything seemed to be ten times more complicated than it needed to be."

Morris lifts my hand to his mouth and plants a kiss on the back of it. My skin tingles at the friction of his scruff.

We ride a ways more in silence, but I notice Morris's hand goes a little bit lax holding mine. He pulls away and starts holding the steering wheel with both hands. He's checking and rechecking the mirrors and changing lanes.

"Morris, what is it?" I ask. I peek into the passenger side mirror to see if there's a problem. "Are we being followed?"

Morris nods. "I think so. Not sure." His lips are a

thin line, and I can tell he's squinting by the crinkles around the side of his eye barely visible with his sunglasses.

Before I can twist in my seat and look behind us, I hear the chirp of a siren and see flashing lights behind us.

"Okay, okay." Morris lifts a hand and waves it, then signals and pulls off to the side of the same busy highway where just a day ago my car stalled. "Let's see what this is all about."

"Were you speeding?" I ask. There's a Florida Highway Patrol car behind us, and a uniformed officer is sitting behind the wheel, fully stopped.

"No," Morris says. "I wasn't."

We watch in the rearview as the officer gets out of the vehicle and walks up to the rear of the truck. He looks at the back of the SUV and sets a hand on the rear driver's side door. He stays there a moment, peering into the windows.

"What's he doing?" I ask. "Looking for something? Why is he touching the car?"

Morris cracks a smile. "Haven't you ever been pulled over, darlin'? Cops leave their prints on cars when they make a traffic stop alone. That way, if I pull out a weapon, shoot, and flee, he's left some evidence on my car that will help them find me."

"Oh my God," I say. "Is that true?"

He nods. "And since we're in an SUV, he's taking his time coming to the window to see if he can make out movement, anybody hidden in the back seat or on the floor. Any suspicious or unusual movements."

"Jesus." My heart rate picks up, not because we're doing anything wrong, but because all of a sudden, it feels like we're in trouble. And we haven't even done anything. I can't imagine how people like this officer put his life on the line every day like this.

What if we were bad guys fleeing a crime?

What if we were doing something illegal?

The idea makes me feel vaguely sick. The reality of the danger, of the risk, feels all too personal.

"Hands on the dash, darlin'," Morris says. He rolls down both of our windows all the way and puts both hands on the steering wheel at ten and two, just like they teach in driver's ed, and he nods at me to put my hands on the dash in full view of the approaching officer.

The officer steps up to the window, and I notice Morris nod.

"Good morning, Officer." Morris smiles.

"License and registration," the officer barks at us, not a greeting, not a kind note in his voice.

"Yes, sir," Morris says. "Happy to do that. My license is in my wallet, which is in my jeans pocket here. May I grab that for you, sir? My girl can pull my insurance and registration from the glove box when you say it's all right."

The cop points a finger at Morris. "Step out of the car, sir. You can get your wallet while keeping your hands in my line of sight. Miss," he barks at me, "I'm gonna ask you not to move until I tell you to."

I swallow hard against the thudding of my pulse in my throat. What the hell did we do? Why is he acting like we robbed a bank?

While I sit there and try not to burst into tears, Morris negotiates every move he makes out of the truck, answering questions about whether he has any weapons or drugs in the car or on his person. Thankfully, the answer to all of that is no. I strain to hear what the officer says, but I keep my hands fixed on the dash while he runs Morris's license and radios in.

The next thing I know, he's got Morris in cuffs, and he's sitting on the curb. The officer comes around to the passenger side window and starts barking questions.

"Ma'am, what's your name?"

"Do you want to see the registration?" I ask, confused for a moment.

"Ma'am! I asked you a question! What's your name?"

I tell him my name as my voice shakes. I have no fucking idea what's going on here. "Officer, what's wrong? What did we do?"

"Do you have any identification on you?" he asks, ignoring my questions.

I take my lead from Morris and politely ask the officer if I can get my driver's license from my purse.

He agrees and watches me open my purse, pull out my wallet, and hand over my license. He checks it over carefully, and then he leans close to me.

"Ma'am, who is this man to you?" The officer's tone hasn't lightened up at all. "How do you know this man?"

"Morris?" I ask. "Morris is my…my boyfriend. Why?" I ask. "What's going on? I don't understand!"

"Your boyfriend," he says, shaking his head. "Ma'am, I'm going to have to ask you to get out of the car. I'm going to put your boyfriend in the squad car, and then I'm going to ask you a few questions. You're not in trouble, but I'm going to need you to do exactly as I say."

"I don't understand!" I'm confused and crying now, the tears running down my face.

As the officer moves Morris into the back of his car, a second and then a third police car pull up and create a formation around us, blocking us in. I wish I could call someone, or at least talk to Morris.

Does he have some kind of warrant out there that I don't know about? Does he have some shady criminal past that's just now coming back to bite him? Why the fuck is this happening?

Once Morris is secured in the first car and all the officers are surrounding us, a female officer approaches me.

"Alice Sparrow?"

I nod. I still have my hands on the dash, and tears and snot are running down my face.

I follow the officer's instructions to the letter. I get out of the car and keep my hands where they can see them. They separate me from Morris, and when I try to look back at him, the female officer yells at me to look straight down and not back.

I sit on the curb where they tell me to sit, out of sight of Morris in the squad car. I have never been so terrified in my life. I've never had a ticket. I've never been pulled over. I have never so much as had a detention before, so I'm completely unprepared for this.

I'm afraid. I'm angry. And I'm thoroughly confused. That is, until the female officer approaches me and starts asking questions.

"Why did you tell us your name was Alice Sparrow, Mrs. Cruz?"

I'm stunned by that. I've never taken Jerry's last name. Since he didn't plan to adopt Zoey, I wanted to share the same last name with my daughter. That was the name on my license and everything legal… I just…

Oh fuck.

Now the pieces are starting to fall into place.

That motherfucker Jerry.

CHAPTER
TWENTY-TWO

MORRIS

THIS HAS BEEN one of the most awful fucking days ever. When I get my hands on that motherfucker Jerry Cruz, and I will someday, I will make sure when I'm done with him, he can't tell his mouth from his asshole and his asshole from his ear. And after that, I'll make sure he never has the use of his natural teeth again.

It takes the rest of the goddamn day to sort out the bullshit with the police. Alice's douchebag husband filed a missing persons report and a missing child report on Alice and Zoey.

It took the entire day of giving statements, providing documents and evidence, and explaining the situation to the cops before they agreed to let us go. But the worst of all was Alice and I had to ride with the cops to the shop to show them that Zoey was indeed alive and well and in the care of friends entrusted by her mother.

Thank God Alice had Zoey's birth certificate on her, as well as a passport. Since she plans to enroll Zoey in a new school, she'd brought all the paperwork she needed to assure the police that the girl was who we said she was and that Alice was her sole parent and legal guardian. She never planned to go back to Jerry's house, so she'd taken absolutely everything. But that motherfucker didn't bother mentioning that all Alice's personal paperwork was missing when he called the cops.

Since Jerry never adopted Zoey, he was smart about that call. He didn't make a familial abduction report, but he was able to claim that he wasn't able to reach his wife or her daughter and that he was in grave fear for their safety since they never got on the flight they'd planned for their spring break. As far as Jerry knew, his wife met some unknown fate and never made it on that plane to Denver.

He reported that she left for a vacation with her daughter, but when she never got on the flight, he drove to the airport parking lot and found her car.

When he went into the car, he found Zoey's iPad under the driver's side seat turned off and their luggage, packed full of their clothes, in the back. He hadn't heard back from Alice. Rayne, her sister, seemed as confused about what was happening as

Jerry was. And Jerry knew Alice's phone was either turned off or dead.

Dead is what it was, smashed under the heel of my boot when that fucker tried to stalk her using it. But of course, he couldn't know that.

After a day without word from his wife and her daughter, he called the police and made the report.

Coincidentally, and I say that with air quotes around it, not long after the report was taken by local authorities in Miami, a tip was called in to the Florida state police saying that a woman who matched Alice's description was spotted in a truck.

And yeah, they managed to catch the license plate.

My license plate.

That fucker Jerry knew exactly what he was doing.

Alice begged the police to take some kind of action against Jerry for filing a false missing persons report, but they claimed they couldn't.

Technically, since Alice had never texted or called Jerry back, he had no way of knowing she wasn't actually missing or in danger.

The police told us they would close their report and notify the spouse that Alice had been located and had left of her own accord.

But the fucking salt in the wound of all this was that there would be no penalty for Jerry. He caused us a day of stress and inconvenience. And there wasn't a goddamn thing I could do to vent out the rage that rose through my chest like steam.

The good news, if there was any, was that since we technically didn't do anything wrong, we weren't in trouble. Small fucking favors.

The cops gave Alice some pamphlets about domestic violence and offered some social services for Zoey, all of which she politely declined for now.

But being off the hook with the cops didn't do jack shit to ease my full-body rage.

"That motherfucker's gonna pay," I seethe. It's nearly sundown by the time we're all back at the building.

Lia and Leo have taken care of Zoey all day, and all of us are tired and out of sorts. Alice has been alternating between crying and cursing a blue streak. Rage, sadness, guilt. It's been a charged day, and all we want is to get the fuck back to Leo's, have a meal, and put this goddamn day in the rearview.

The only ones who seem completely unfazed are Lia and Zoey.

"Check it out, Mama. The puppies are on TV." Zoey came running through the grassy lot to greet us.

We've barely parked the truck in front of the building when her glittery shoes come running from inside one of the middle storefront doors.

Leo is working in the repair bay with all the doors open, and Lia trails a few steps behind Zoey, closing the door to the store, leaving her girl crew of dogs inside.

"Yeah, baby. That's great." Alice manages a weak smile and gives Zoey a hug.

"No, look. Mama, you have to look! We made a puppy cam!" Zoey holds up a glittery pink cell phone and swipes at the screen.

Alice peers down at the image. "Wow, honey." She studies the images, and I look over her shoulder.

I can somehow see the dogs that are still inside the store in a window on this glittery pink phone.

"That's so cool," Alice continues. "How did you do that?"

"Lia has a hotpot."

Alice looks completely perplexed.

"Lia has an internet *hotspot*." Leo comes out from the repair bay to translate.

"I use it on the road to make sure I can get a signal even when I can't get a signal," Lia explains. "The device itself is really cheap, and I have internet everywhere I go as long as the little guy is charged up."

Lia walks us into the middle unit in my strip mall and points to a tiny black device plugged into the wall. It's no bigger than an old-school alarm clock, but apparently that's not the only thing she's set up. There are two small wireless cameras turned inward on the store.

"When you look at this app on your phone, you're

seeing the image or video that these cameras pick up. You can flip views and see the dogs playing, turn on the volume and actually hear if they're barking. You can even talk to the dogs through the app from wherever you are." Lia bends down in front of one of the cameras, and the view instantly changes into a giant image of her smile. "So, if we need to leave the dogs alone, we can keep them here and just check up on them by checking the app. When they can't be with me, of course. And if we're here playing with the dogs, you can use the app to peek in on us. Sort of like a nanny cam. I set up the app on the extra phone for you, Alice."

Alice looks exhausted, but she manages a smile for the girl. "Thank you. That's actually really sweet."

Lia and Zoey high-five each other. "Team Girl Crew goes viral."

Leo walks up to me. "Since I have internet at the house, Lia said we could leave the hotspot here for the time being. You'll want to get a real internet package for this place eventually. But for now, while the place is still unoccupied a lot of the time, I thought you'd like to make sure your stuff stays secure." Leo gives me a small grin. "Our stuff. You know, until my grandpa's truck is drivable."

Leo shows me a couple of discreet freestanding cameras he's placed facing his grandpa's car, the dumpster out back, and then facing the front door.

"I only bought three cameras, but they're motion

activated. They sit idle until anything moves, and then if something passes in front of it and triggers the sensor, the camera takes a picture and sends it to your phone. So, if it's a raccoon or something, you'll get a notice that there's a big-ass—*butt*." He steals a quick look at Zoey. "A big-*butt* raccoon walking around. It will take a picture and send it to the app. All you have to do is check the notifications and see what's what. It's not a replacement for a full security system, but it'll do in a pinch. We can cover the truck, the dumpster, and the main door for the time being."

I'm awed by this technology and how much these kids know. I motion to the phone Lia has handed to Alice. "Can I check out the app?"

"I can install it on your phone," Leo says. "No reason why we can't all be on it. It's free. The only thing we pay for are the cameras, which I bought with some of the leftover cash you gave me for the parts for Alice's car." Leo looks at me. "I didn't think you'd mind, especially if Lia and Zoey are going to be spending some time here."

I nod. "You did good, kid. Real good."

"Alice might want to limit her view to only the doggie day care room, or she can just silence the notifications and only check the app when she's not with Zoey. Or, we can all keep tabs on the shop and the dogs," he explains.

"Think we need something like this for the house?" I ask. "With the ladies and all…" I catch myself and backpedal a bit. "You know, we should probably work out just how long this arrangement at your place is going to last. And I need a good meal and a couple of good drinks before I get into anything else serious tonight."

Leo nods. "Look, Morris. You've given me work, you're making all my meals, and I haven't had this much fun in a long time. We're good. You all are welcome to stay. We'll figure it out. Just promise me you'll bring me back to the compound someday. Maybe let me buy you a beer and talk about the MC when all the dust settles."

I nod and wish I had the energy to give the kid a clap on the back. But right now, I'm exhausted and pissed off as fuck. I want a hot meal, a hot shower, and a hot little bird straddling my lap. Everything else can wait.

The mood in the house is a lot more somber tonight, but Zoey and Lia do their part to brighten us up.

While the girls reclaim the slumber party room, making some such origami paper nonsense, spreading markers and colored papers all over Leo's floor, Leo sits on the couch with a beer, playing on his phone while he pretends not to moon over Lia.

The big dog has claimed Leo's lap, and the three

humans and three dogs fill out the living room while Alice and I take over the kitchen.

"Want some help?" I ask. I've just taken a long hot shower, and I'm feeling slightly more human. Still homicidal toward Jerry fucking Cruz, but more human.

Alice sighs lightly and turns to face me. She's chopping veggies for a stir-fry and is nursing a beer. Her feet are bare, and she's pulled her hair into a messy bun while she cooks. She turns to face me, and I see something in her has changed.

"Morris," she says. "I'm so, so sorry." But Alice doesn't sound sorry. She sounds pissed. "What happened today was all my fault."

I pull open the fridge and grab a bottle of beer, then take a seat at the table. "Stop that talk. This was a dick move by Jerry. He knew goddamned well what he was doing. The kind of trouble he was going to cause. This isn't your fault at all. He filed that report. He wanted to see you sweat."

"No," she says, sounding more resolute. "Today is totally on me." She sets the knife down on the cutting board and joins me at the table. "Morris, if I hadn't been too afraid to leave Jerry, if I had just filed for divorce, served him with the papers while he was at work, fought him for the house and his businesses…"

"If you did that, you might be dead right now," I say, shaking my head. "Alice, everybody knows the most dangerous time in an abusive relationship is when the spouse being abused decides to leave. You know this asshole. You knew he wasn't going to let you go easy. Now we all know it. You did the right thing. The only thing you could do."

She presses her lips into a thin line. "You know what's funny?" she asks. "I was scared today. Really scared. More scared than I have ever been by anything he's ever done. And I know that's what he wanted. He feels powerful when I'm afraid. Or weak. Or vulnerable."

"Typical bully," I say. "Tale as old as time."

"But now, I'm not afraid," she admits. "I'm fucking furious." She scoots her chair closer to me and explains. Our knees touch under the table, and even though I can smell the rice she's put on the stove starting to boil, I lean forward and give her all my attention. "All I could think about today," she says, "was protecting you."

"Protecting me?"

She nods. "You mean everything to me. I don't know how to explain it, but the only thing that ran through my head when I wasn't sure what was happening was that I would do anything—anything—to protect you. I wasn't sure if you had a warrant out for your arrest or if you were some kind of criminal. But once I stopped being scared and I thought about who you are, what I feel for you... I know it may seem crazy after such a short time, but all I cared about was making it okay for you. Making the fear stop. I didn't want anything bad to happen to you."

I lean across the table and kiss her lips. I open my mouth and taste the beer mixed with her natural sugary sweetness. "Baby, you never have to protect me."

She nods. "But I wanted to. I knew we were being treated unfairly. I just didn't realize why until later. We were being bullied by Jerry, and the police were just pawns, being manipulated by him. What a waste. A waste of police resources. A waste of our time. I was scared, but now I'm so ashamed."

"The only thing that stops a bully is someone standing up to them," I say. "And bullies…they feed off people's fear and their shame. If Jerry didn't have the power to make you feel those things, he'd have no power over you at all."

"Together, we're the only thing that Jerry can't beat," she says. Alice looks determined as she reaches across the table for my hand and squeezes. "After our night together, all I could think about was that I was doing it again," she admitted.

"Doing what?" I ask.

"Running to a man to save me. First, I tried to lose myself in Zoey's dad and sex. Then, it was Jerry, bailing me out of my single-mother hell. Now, it's you. All morning, I was sure I'd made a huge mistake and that you'd figure out soon enough that you did too.

Either I'd want to leave you, or you'd want to leave me."

I shake my head. "Sweetheart, you don't know me very well yet, although you should." I give her a saucy wink. "I'm in this thing. You've had my heart since I saw you in that gas station. I just didn't know it right away. Want to make you my old lady. Make this shit official."

"Old lady?" she asks, looking confused and a little insulted.

"It's a thing. All the brothers call their women old ladies. It's like a term of endearment all the bikers use."

She gives me a wry smile. "Old lady. So, we spend one night together, and we fly through the courting and the dating. I'm an old lady after just one night."

After the day we've had, it feels like we've spent a lifetime together. But I know this is only the start of what we can have. Of what we can share. Of more.

"It doesn't matter how long it's been," I tell her. "I just know."

"Morris," she says, squeezing my bicep with her tiny hand. "You sound like a greeting card."

"So?" I say, leaning close to her. "I'm a man of many talents. Many, many talents. Talents which I hope to share with you again and again. All night long, specifically. Now, let's eat dinner so you and I can go to bed."

CHAPTER
TWENTY-THREE

ALICE

DINNER IS QUIET TONIGHT.

Leo looks at the sautéed kale like it's raw gator meat, but when he sees Lia noshing on it, he gives it a try. After chewing and chewing and chewing, I see him slip the whole bite into a napkin, but I know he's not insulting my cooking.

Zoey chatters away happily about the origami project. She and Lia are making a string of paper cranes that they plan to hang with a strand of fairy lights to create a "magical backyard girl crew garden" or something like that.

I love that Lia seems completely content to hang out and work on crafts. I don't know what the girl's dreams or plans for her future are, but she's a great influence on Zoey. Sweet, good-natured, and great manners.

I wonder how she and Tiny will be over time. I think about Zoey growing up without a dad for so long, and then having Jerry as the male influence in her life. She's going to need a lot of Morris and Leo time to undo the damage Jerry's done. Even just a few days away from Jerry's rules and temper seem to have made my little princess a lot more open, less restrained. Less shy.

A few days away from Jerry have done the same for me. I still don't have money, a job, or a plan, but something has changed for me. I'm different.

I watch the people eating around the table, the delicious smells of my chicken stir-fry still filling the kitchen. Lia's dogs have eaten their herbal smoothie doggie dinners and are lazing on the kitchen floor near the back door.

I clear the dishes from the table, excusing everyone else to go get comfortable and relax while I clean.

Only Morris stays behind.

He watches me while I wash the dishes, the hot soapy water relaxing my hands and giving my mind something familiar to focus on. I know Jerry isn't gone. I haven't fully put the nightmare behind me. But tonight, I can dream of something more.

People I love around me.

Work I care about.

A place to live filled with laughter.

The past in the rearview.

A life I choose.

* * *

After I tuck Zoey in, I take a shower to wash the pains of the day away, then climb into bed beside Morris.

"I love everybody in this house."

"You love everybody under this roof, huh?" Morris is shirtless and wearing sleep pants. His feet are bare, and he's on top of the covers. He's wearing a pair of reading glasses, and he's looking at something on his phone.

"Yeah, Professor, I do," I say, tapping the stem of his glasses. "You look hot in these. Sexy."

"Necessity," he explains. "The perils of being an old man. But I love the compliment, sweetheart."

"What are the perils of being an old lady?" I ask. "Specifically, your old lady?"

Morris gives me a smile and pulls the glasses from his face. "I don't know about perils, but there are definitely some perks."

"Really?" I ask. "Like…?"

Morris sets his phone on the bedside table and looks me over. His expression is wicked, teasing. A dimple blooms in the corner of his cheek when he gives me that naughty, seductive smile, and I want to lick my way from the scruff on his neck until I can taste that sweet spot on his cheek.

"Happy to show you," he says. He touches my chin with a finger and draws me close to his face.

Once his lips touch mine, the flirtation falls away and I cling to him. I want to lose this shitty day, bury it in the pleasure of Morris's touch. I want to feel every hard angle and plane of his body beneath me, feel the bite of his teeth tearing deliciously against the flesh of my thighs.

"Morris," I whisper. "I want you so badly. It almost scares me. This hunger. It's like I'll never be satisfied."

"I love a hungry woman," he growls. "As long as the only meal you ever need is right here." He points to himself, his hand motioning toward his already-hard cock.

"And here," I add, taking his hand from his dick and moving it toward his heart. "I want both. And more. This," I say and lean forward to kiss his forehead. "And here." I kiss his neck.

I work my way down his body, kissing the planes of his smooth chest, the contours of his sculpted abs. His cock bobs invitingly under his pajamas, and I kiss closer and closer until finally my mouth is over his dick, and I'm breathing hot kisses through his pants.

"Fuck, woman," he hisses, clenching the covers with his hands. "The things you do with that mouth."

"The things I will do," I correct. I slide two fingers under the waistband of his pants and shift them down just far enough that his cock springs free. He groans, and I hold the pants out of the way with my hand, leaving them on, but paying lavish attention to his generous length.

I plant featherlight kisses on the shaft and puff out hot little breaths as I work up his anticipation for the heat of my mouth. When the tip is weeping and his chest is rising and falling in erratic breaths, I sink my lips onto his cock, drawing the length of him into my mouth with a firm, deep suck.

He gasps but then quickly relaxes, his face composed, but his lower lip clamped between his teeth.

"Alice," he grinds out.

But I hold up a finger to shush him. I want this to be about him. He's done so much for me, and I'm sure if last night was any indication, I'll wake up in the middle of the night to a sweet surprise and a flood of orgasms. But right now, I want to take care of him. I want to taste him, feel him, explore his body and everything that makes him feel good. I want to treat my old man like a true old lady would. Pleasing him. Loving him.

I move to kneel over his legs and get into a better position to hold his dick in my hand and suck him in, when all of a sudden, both of our phones start to chirp.

"What's that?" I wonder, lifting my head up.

"Ignore it," he mumbles, not even opening his eyes.

But the sound is insistent, and it's coming from both of our phones. "Morris, something isn't right." I reach over and pull the waistband of his pants to cover his cock, and I turn to find the pink glitter phone Lia gave me earlier.

The moment broken, Morris's brow furrows as he grabs his phone too. "What the fuck is this?" he mutters. "I have never heard this noise before."

"It's an app notification," I say, swiping at the home screen to bring up all the recent notifications. But I don't have to struggle to figure it out. I hear a set of pounding footsteps on the stairs and the sound of a door opening.

"Morris?"

"Alice!"

Leo and Lia are both at the door, knocking and calling our names.

"Come in," I call, and Morris tosses a pillow over his lap to hide his arousal.

Leo shoves open the door. His face is white, and Lia is holding her phone out to us to see.

"The cameras," she explains. "Something set off the motion sensors. There's a picture."

So, that's what it is. The motion sensor doggie cam app Leo and Lia installed on our phones.

"What is it?" Morris asks.

Lia looks at him gravely as she shows him a photo the app captured. "It's a man, Morris. There's someone in the building."

I look at the image on Lia's phone and then quickly look at the one I'm holding in my hand. It's not just any man inside the building.

It's Jerry Cruz.

CHAPTER
TWENTY-FOUR
MORRIS

"STAY WITH THE GIRLS," I bark, leaping out of bed.

"No, Morris. No!" Alice is scrambling out of bed, fumbling for her jeans.

"He's close, and he doesn't know we've seen him." I look to Leo. "Does he? Can he see the cameras?"

"I don't know," Leo admits. "I could watch him on the cameras, but the little light on the front of them might turn green if I'm watching. Right now, it's a solid red dot, just like any other appliance. I'm pretty sure if he's looking around with a flashlight, he's seen the cameras. I can't say for sure."

"I need to go." I'm already dressed, and my phone's in my pocket. "I can make it to the building in less than ten minutes. Alice, stay here with your daughter. It's not safe. Let me handle this."

"Fuck that!" Alice shocks me and, by the looks of

it, Leo and Lia too. "This is my husband, and you're my boyfriend…old man…whatever! I want to see this through, Morris. No more running."

I nod. "Let's earn your patch, sweetheart." I point to Leo. "You, stay here. I'm counting on you to keep Lia and Zoey safe. We don't know what this asshole's got planned, but if he knows where the building is, you can be damned sure he knows how to find this house." I take Leo's shoulder in my hand and pull him close. "Keep. Them. Safe. I'm counting on you."

Leo's eyes are wide, but his lips are set in a determined line. "I will, man. You can count on me. Do you want me to call 9-1-1?"

"Not yet," I say, shaking my head. "I want that cocksucker all to myself first."

I fly toward the building, not giving a shit if I get pulled over for speeding. At this hour, I'll risk it. I know whatever he's planning, he's likely doing alone, so my best hope is for the element of surprise. I cut the lights on the truck as I slow.

I can see a car parked off to the far side of the lot, almost hidden in the unlit tree line. I pull over right next to the car, blocking it in as best I can with my truck. He'll be able to get around me, but that's only if he makes it back to his car.

As soon as I park, I see the orange. Flames.

"Jerry!" Alice is out of the car in a flash, screaming at the top of her lungs. "You motherfucking asshole, you set a fire!"

I can't see shit, but since I know he's gotta still be here, I turn the wheel of the truck and flip the headlights on high beam.

The building isn't engulfed in flames, but it looks like there are two fires. One coming from inside one of the storefronts, and a smaller one that lights up the night sky from someplace behind the building.

Then it hits me.

It can only be one thing.

Leo's grandpa's truck.

Alice disappears in the dark, running toward the fire and screaming bloody murder for Jerry to come out. I dial 9-1-1 and report the fire, giving them the address of this place. I tell them it's arson, and the suspect is still on the property, that we caught him in the act. Then I drop my phone, because I know damn well I've got a matter of minutes before law enforcement arrives. And if I have any hope of tearing this motherfucker's face off and calling it self-defense, I've got probably three minutes to find him.

But I don't have to look too hard. I hear screams and the sounds of a violent struggle coming from behind the building.

I race back there and see Alice holding a two-by-four she must have picked up from someplace near the dumpster. She's swinging it like a baseball bat and swearing.

"I'm gonna kill you, you bitch," Jerry says. "And your filthy loser boyfriend. And then I'm gonna find your no-good kid, and I'm gonna tell her what a goddamn whore of a mother she had!"

Alice runs full speed toward Jerry, swinging the board toward his face.

"I dare you, Jerry, you piece-of-shit coward. I never loved you. I've always hated you! Now, come here and try to hurt me. You just try, you worthless piece of shit!"

She races toward him again and again, lurching and swinging, but she misses every time. He dodges and weaves away, but he stays close enough to taunt her with more threats.

"Fuck you and your sister and your friends and your goddamn daughter!" His words are ugly, and they match his face, twisted and mottled in the blazing light from the fires.

I hear sirens in the distance, and I know we're out of time. Almost.

Jerry hasn't seen me yet, so I creep quietly around the burning truck and come up from behind him. Alice sees me approach but doesn't say a word. She keeps screaming at him, swearing, and swinging her makeshift bat at his face.

"Fuck you!" she screams again. "I hate you!"

Jerry does the thing then that will be his undoing.

He races forward and slaps Alice, full on the face. He lands a perfect blow that sends her staggering backward. She drops the board and falls to her knees, gripping her face in her hands.

"Big mistake, fuckwad," I say. Just as Jerry straightens and pulls his hand back to land another blow, I grab it, twist it, and hear the crack that lets me know his poor little arm won't be striking my baby ever again.

He shrieks like a cat whose tail's been run over by a car. "You fucking broke my arm! I'm pressing charges, you goddamn maniac! You broke my arm!"

"You hit my baby, you motherfucking douchebag," I say, making sure to twist his arm a little harder to drive home the point. "And you're burning down my building. So, I think the charges that are going be filed are gonna be against you."

"Fuck you!" Jerry tries to wrestle away from me, but all he can do is shriek in pain every time he moves.

"Alice," I call calmly. "Baby, are you okay? I don't really wanna let this guy go before the cops get here. Can you reach your two-by-four?"

Alice is standing up, and while it guts me to see, blood drips down the side of her face where Jerry hit her and his ring cut her cheek. But the look on her face leaves no room for sympathy. No room for worry. Alice's face is a mask of raw emotion. Rage. Fury. White-hot anger.

She nods and grabs the board from the ground, staggering forward, her eyes looking from Jerry's dick to his face. I love this woman. She's actually trying to decide where to land her blow.

"Take your shot while you've got it, baby," I say. "Time's running out."

The flames are crawling toward the stars, and the sirens are growing louder and longer. Help is close.

Then Alice does something that surprises me. She drops the board. She walks up to Jerry and looks him in the eye. Her face is sweating and bloody, her hair stained red and mangled from the furious swings she took at him earlier.

She watches Jerry, evaluating her move, and as much as I want to twist—just one more flick of my wrist and I'll nearly tear the dude's arm off—I don't. Something in me holds back. Knows that this moment is between Alice and her tormentor. This moment belongs to her.

"Fuck you, Jerry. I hope you rot." She steps slightly away from us and kicks him as hard as she can in the junk.

I almost feel the impact of her kick in *my* nuts. Jerry screams like a bitch and drops to his knees. The pressure on his arm, which I still hold firm in my hands, causes a second agonizing scream to tear from his lips.

"Sorry, babe," Alice says, her voice caustic with

sarcasm. "But I learned it's a lot better to never leave a mark." She shrugs. "Then there's no proof."

Jerry is coughing and dry heaving, rolling on the ground when the fire trucks arrive. A squad car isn't far behind, and they take Jerry into custody while the fire marshal takes Alice and me aside to ask some questions. She pulls out the app on her phone and shows them the still images the doggie cams caught. Jerry sneaking into the property. Trashing the inside of the stores. And then setting fire to the building, Leo's truck, and even the dumpster, but that stupid motherfucker couldn't get the dumpster to ignite. That extra couple minutes he struggled to set fire to the dumpster are probably what kept him there long enough for us to catch him in the act.

Serves him right.

The photos seem to be all the evidence they need. When they take Jerry away on a stretcher, he's accompanied by two cops and handcuffed to the gurney.

CHAPTER
TWENTY-FIVE
MORRIS

"PRINCESS ZOEY! Come on, you're gonna be late for your first day of school." Lia scurries around the kitchen, holding two of her dogs. "I can't find your lunch. Did you already put your lunch in your backpack?"

"I did." Alice hands Lia the brand-new princess backpack, complete with a new, soft-sided lunchbox.

"Mommy!" Zoey skids into the kitchen on her favorite pair of glitter shoes. "Do we have time for Lia to braid feathers into my hair?"

Alice chuckles and checks the time. "Not this morning, sweetheart. Let's leave something special for your second day at the new school, okay?"

Leo fills a travel mug with coffee and grabs a banana from a bowl of fruit on the counter. "See you around ten?" he asks.

I nod. "We'll be there. If the insurance people get

there before I do, just get started without me. You know the property even better than I do."

After the fire was put out and Jerry was arrested and charged with arson, we got Zoey enrolled in school and filed a claim with the insurance company to get the building repaired. Since most of the contents had been pulled out before the closing, all the fire damage was minimal. The walls and floors needed tearing out, but we would have replaced that anyway. Thankfully, the insurance money will help pay to restore some of Leo's grandfather's truck too.

"Start without you. Got it, boss." Leo nods and ruffles Zoey's hair as he says goodbye. "Have a great first day, princess."

"Leo," Zoey groans. "Don't mess up my hair. Lia just finished it."

Alice smooths back the hairs Leo messed up, although, to be fair, I think she looks the same as she did. "Okay, my love. Have a great day. I'll see you when you get home from school. Make new friends, don't be shy. And just have fun."

Zoey kisses her mom, then takes Lia's hand as they head out to Tiny's truck. "Shy?" Zoey chatters, tossing her perfect little backpack over her shoulders. "I'm not ever shy. Why would Mama say that?"

Lia waves as they head out, tossing a smile back at us.

Then finally, Alice and I are alone.

I cross the kitchen and pull her against my chest. "Come on," I say. "I've got a surprise for you."

"Mmm, what kind of surprise?" Alice's caramel eyes light up, and her sugar-sweet smile fills my senses as I lean down to kiss her.

"Come on. I'll show you."

I take her hand and lead her through the house, out to Leo's garage. I pop the door and wait for the mechanical slats to slide away, revealing what I've left inside for my sweet little bird.

"Morris?" Alice twirls to face me. "What is this?"

We've been jockeying cars and trucks, depending on what we need, where we need to go, but I've also been parking my motorcycle in Leo's garage. On the ground beside it is a gift-wrapped box.

"That's for you," I say, pointing to the box. "Open it."

While she opens her gift, I watch her. This is the woman I want to make my old lady. The one I want to make memories with, make love to—hell, make something I never thought I'd ever want, but which now I know I need. A family.

"Morris…" Alice turns to face me, her eyes wet with tears. "This is…this is just…"

"You've earned it, baby."

She pulls a brand-new, custom-painted motorcycle helmet from the box. The helmet itself is a perfect shiny black, but inked on the back in smoky gray and red are an enormous pair of wings.

"It's not a patch, but they're yours. Your new set of wings." I help her slide the helmet over her hair and size it to fit.

"Morris, I don't know what to say." Her voice is shaking, and she's smiling through her tears.

"Say you'll go for a ride with me, sweetheart. Say you'll get back up with me, no matter how many times life knocks us down and tries to break us. Say you'll fly with me as long as we both have wings."

She clings to me in a tight hug, made a little awkward by the bulk of the helmet. I laugh and pull a matching one for me from where I hid it behind some of Leo's grandpa's old tools.

"Shall we?" I ask. I hold out a hand to my old lady. We've got close to three hours before my new office manager and I need to be at the property to meet with the insurance people. Plenty of time.

Alice climbs on behind me, and I feel her grip me tight around the waist.

"You scared, baby?"

If the strength of her grip is any indication, she's stain-her-panties terrified. And that's the last thing I want to cause her.

"No." She whispers it against my back.

But I know the truth.

I feel it.

She is afraid, but she trusts me.

She's uncertain how to hold on and trust.

But she is.

She's doing it.

I think back to all the times in her life when she must have been afraid. Facing the future alone with Zoey and no help, no support.

When she realized the man she married was nothing more than a douchebag in a suit. When she made the plan that brought her into my world. The attention and care that went into every detail. She had to be that way. Had to put her little girl first. Had to put her strength and heart and head together and push the terror away.

I climb off the bike and check the time on my phone.

"What is it?" Alice looks concerned. "Did I say something wrong?"

I shake my head and reach for her hand. "Nope," I tell her. "And let's get one thing straight. You never have to worry about saying anything wrong to me."

Alice's nostrils flare as she takes in a deep breath. She's listening to my words, but her eyes sear into mine. She's thinking fast, wondering what I'm thinking. What I want.

The last thing I want is for this thing between us to remind her of anything she's been through before. That fucker Cruz. That loser whose name I don't even need to know, the jizz-stain that brought beautiful Zoey into the world.

"Come here," I say.

Alice steps off the bike and removes her helmet

before she steps close to me. "What is it, Morris?" she asks, her caramel eyes going dark.

I reach past her and click the button on the wall that closes the garage door behind us.

"Morris?" Alice looks confused. "Aren't we going to ride?"

I nod. "Soon. There's something I want to get straight with you first."

Alice meets my eyes, a slight frown tugging her full lips downward. "Okay. What is it?" she asks.

I bend my head to hers and kiss her lips lightly.

"Cruz was the last worthless motherfucker to lay his hands on you," I grit out against her lips. "From now on, if I touch you, it's because you want it so badly, you're begging for it. If you've got something to say, you fucking say it. You wanna call me a no-good motherfucker because I didn't take out the trash, you do it."

I lift her chin and meet her questioning stare.

"Alice," I say before sweeping her mouth with my tongue. "I'm not expecting you to trust me overnight, to put the past completely behind you. But I want you to try. No fear. Between you and me, there's none of that old shit. You wanna walk away from me, you walk. You wanna run toward me, you climb aboard and ride me hard. We clear?"

Alice swallows. She blinks at me, a shimmer of tears making me unsure whether she's happy or sad. I'm not left wondering what's behind the look for long, though. Alice leans close and rests a palm against my chest.

"We're clear," she says. "And Morris?"

I nod.

"Thank you." Alice rests her forehead against me, and I wrap my hands around her waist.

"Nothing to thank me for, darlin'," I say. I'm about to climb back on the bike so we can get this ride underway when Alice stops me.

"Nobody's home," she whispers against me, a puff of sugary sweetness reaching my nose. "And we have a little time…"

"Yeah? What'd you have in mind?"

My sweet little bird steps away from me and gives me a saucy lift of one eyebrow. "There's another kind of ride I'd like to take on this bike," she says.

I like the way this woman thinks.

I nod and cross my arms over my chest as Alice slips her hands under her tank top. She shrugs the fabric over her shoulders and stands before me in another pair of those ass-hugging yoga pants and a whisper-thin bra. Her nipples bead up as I stare at them, almost like they know what my mouth has in store.

"Mmm-hmm," I mutter, trying hard to let her take the lead. Everything in me wants to grab her hips, turn her over my bike, and show her all the ways I want to ride. But this moment is about our connection. About Alice leading the way. About Alice learning to trust me. And that's a lesson I'm more than happy to wait for.

Alice reaches behind her and unclasps her bra with a single satisfying snap. Her firm tits are free, and the warm air in the garage pebbles her skin. Her eyes blaze, and I know she wants to know how I feel about what I'm seeing. She wants encouragement, and fuck, how I want to give it to her.

"Fuck me, Alice," I say. "Your body…your smile…"

Before the words are out, she's completely naked, standing before me looking proud and not even a little shaky.

"What are you waiting for?" she asks, a tease in her voice. "That belt won't unbuckle itself."

I waste no time freeing my dick from the confines of my jeans. Alice doesn't even wait for me to step out of them. She turns and bends deep at the waist, supporting her weight on the seat of my bike. As she tries to settle herself so the bike doesn't tip over, she starts cracking up.

"This sounded a lot sexier than it seems to be turning out," she says.

"This is very fucking sexy," I assure her. "But let's make sure we don't tip over. A sex accident in his garage would be real awkward to explain to Leo tonight."

Still wearing my shirt, I step out of my jeans so I can walk Alice's naked body toward the wall of the garage. Leo's got tools hanging on hooks, but there are more than enough places where Alice can brace herself with her tiny palms.

She faces the garage wall, and I bury my mouth against her neck, kissing her ears, her hair, and reaching around her to pinch those tight nipples until she purrs. She widens her stance, opening her legs and jutting her ass up against me.

"Morris," she begs. "Please."

I angle my cock against her ass and work my hips so the head slides smooth as satin between her thighs. She wobbles as if her knees are weak, and I move my hands to her hips. She gasps, then gives a little disappointed groan when I move my hands from her tits, but she won't be wanting for long.

I slide myself against her lips, teasing her folds with my dick until she's writhing, her hips working hard against me to angle her ass to feel more of my cock. I know she wants me inside. I want to feel her electric tremors beneath me as I make her come, but I want her to enjoy this. I want to take my time, taking her from slick and ready to drenched and desperate.

I keep hold of her hip with one hand, but with the other, I reach between us and press my thumb against her puckered opening. I apply the slightest pressure as I slide inside her pussy, and the guttural moan that erupts from Alice nearly makes me blow right there. I press just the tip of my thumb against her asshole while my dick slides inside, the delicious wetness I find there so slippery, I have to control my movements so I don't slip out.

Within seconds, we've hit our groove, and Alice grinds backward against me, seeking her pleasure against my body while I hold off as long as I can. The animalistic slap of my body against hers is like heaven, and finally, when Alice's nails scratch against the drywall and she heaves huge gasping sighs of bliss, I can release hard and deep inside her.

After we finish, we stay locked together and lean against the garage wall, panting and misted with sweat. I lift the hair from her neck and rest my face in the valley between her shoulders, deeply breathing her now-familiar fragrance.

"Should we clean up?" Alice asks after a minute.

I nod, my legs weak from fucking her standing, my heart rate still slowing. I don't want to leave the erotic fog, but we've got places to be. And more riding to do. Alice pulls on her clothes, and then we both go back inside to quickly wash up. Alice changes into a clean pair of panties, and we head back to the garage.

"Alice Sparrow, my beautiful little bird." I pull on my helmet and reach a hand out to her. "Come on. Let's take a ride."

EPILOGUE
ALICE

EIGHT MONTHS LATER...

"Hey, hey!" Lia says, brushing past me, her cheeks flushed and happy.

There is a weird energy in the air between them, something I can't quite make out, but it started shortly after we moved out of Leo's and into Morris's apartment. I try to catch Leo's eye, because he tends to be a lot more open than Lia, but he's actively avoiding my gaze.

Before I question what's going on, Morris walks in.

"Ho ho ho," he booms, strolling through the door. He is wearing a Santa hat that Zoey made him at school. He looks absolutely gorgeous, silly red cap and all.

I cling to his chest like it's been weeks instead of hours since we last saw each other and lift my face to his for a kiss.

"Hey, baby," he says, waggling his brows at me.

"Nice hat," I tell him.

I know he wears it because Zoey made it for him, the sparkly sequins that spell out his name peeling and falling off, leaving snowy shrapnel on the shoulders of his flannel shirt.

"Okay, let's go," Morris says, motioning with his head toward the door.

"Wait…what? What about dinner?" I look from him to Leo and Lia.

Leo is smiling at me, and Lia has already headed back toward the bedroom, calling for Zoey to bust out her markers and paper.

"We've got crafts to make." Lia's voice sings through the apartment.

I look back at Morris in confusion.

"Trust me, baby?" he asks, as if there's any doubt.

Over the last eight months, Morris has done more to show me that I can trust him than anyone—man, woman, family, or friend—has done in my entire life up until now.

Leo and Lia too. It was great living with them for a short time, but once Jerry was safely behind bars, there was no reason to stay at Leo's. Morris insisted Zoey and I stay at his apartment while he went back to sleeping at the compound almost nightly.

"Of course I do," I say. I grab my purse and a light cardigan. Even though it's December in Florida, when the sun goes down, it gets chilly. "Wait." I put a hand on Morris's arm. "Are we riding or driving?"

He grins. "The sweater will do you just fine, baby. We're taking the truck."

I take Morris's hand and follow him out to the truck. When I climb in the passenger seat, I twist to ask him what we're doing, where we're going, but Morris pulls a face, turns on the ignition, and heads out into the night. I lean back against the seat and enjoy the ride.

Wherever we're going, I know I'm in good hands. The best, actually.

"Morris? Where are we?"

When he pulls the truck up to a small brick building, I can't tell what it is. It's nearly five p.m., and the sun has started sinking in the sky. The violet-colored twilight makes it tough to see any of the signs.

"Come on," he says. He comes around to my side of the truck and opens the door. "There's someone I want you to meet."

I follow Morris into the small building. We ride the elevator to the second floor and head down a quiet, carpeted hallway. The office building needs some work. It looks like a place where shady people have tiny offices to make them look legit. I can't begin to imagine what the hell we're doing here just a few days before Christmas when we've got people back at the apartment, expecting dinner.

Morris knocks on a closed office door, and when it opens, a very old man in an ill-fitting suit answers.

"Morris, you asshole," he says, nodding. His voice sounds like the sputter of a diesel engine. The guy's smoked a lot of cigarettes in his day, if the yellow staining on his thick beard is any indication. His cheeks are heavily pockmarked, but when he looks at me, his smile is wide and sincere. "And you must be Alice."

He reaches out a hand to shake mine, so I extend mine toward him. "Yes," I say. "Nice to meet you…"

"Baby," Morris says, "this is Fingers."

"Fingers," I echo.

The man laughs, a dusty, rattling sound that seems like it might actually be painful. "You can call me Frank, sweetheart. Fingers is my club name. Only the old-timers still call me that."

"Sign of respect, brother," Morris says.

"Frank," I say, "nice to meet you."

Frank's got a hell of a hitch in his step and a deep hunch in his back. I look back at Morris, curious at what the heck is going on, when Frank comes around his desk and motions for us to sit.

"Sweetheart," Morris says, "Fingers here is the club lawyer. He handles any little…scrapes we might get into."

Frank looks at me and clarifies. "Frank

Capobianco, attorney-at-law. I mostly handle criminal cases, thanks to my brothers in the club, but I'm a little bit of a Frank-of-all-trades. I handle real estate and even a bit of family law from time to time."

Morris nods, and Frank pushes a huge stack of papers toward me.

"Okay, young lady," he says, pausing to cough an incredibly dry, raspy round of barks into a stained handkerchief. "'Scuse me. Former smoker. That shit'll kill ya."

He busies himself finding a pen, which you might think a lawyer would have in a drawer or even in a cup on his desk, but finally, he curses and slams a fist down, jostling the stack of papers. "Hang on. Can never find a goddamn pen when you've got a stack of contracts to sign."

"Contracts?" I look at Morris.

Fingers—Frank—is shuffling past us, headed for a small supply closet in one corner of the office. While he audibly curses out everything under the sun as he looks for a new box of pens, Morris shoves a photograph across the desk toward me.

"Merry Christmas, baby." His smile is soft. Tender. Totally unlike my gruff, tattooed biker's normal demeanor. "Bought'cha a little something."

I look down at the picture, and I can hardly process what I'm seeing. "Morris," I say. My hands start to shake as I take it all in. "You bought me...a house?"

Morris nods. "You've got plenty of dough from divorcing the douchebag. You can decorate it, fix it up, make a real home for you and Zoey."

I shake my head, stunned. "Morris, but why? Why would you do this? And what about you?"

I don't get it.

My thoughts race from shock and amazement to confusion. Why would he buy me a house? Doesn't he want to do something like this together? Does he not see some kind of future between us, and this is his way of getting me out of his apartment, and his life?

"Before you think too hard," Morris says, "this is part one of your gift."

"Part one? Of how many?"

"Three," he says. "Now just trust me."

It's hard, but I look Morris in the eye, and I know I have a choice to make. I can doubt his intentions, fear what he's doing, or I can take the pen that Fingers has finally found and sign and initial the contract, binding me to a home I've never even been inside.

Morris looks so delighted, so happy, I can't do anything but sign, sign, sign. When it's all done and I have a fat envelope of paperwork, Morris grabs another envelope from Frank, and they speak in quiet tones before man-hugging each other goodbye.

"Merry Christmas, Alice," Frank says to me as I pull on my sweater. "We'll see each other again in a few weeks to sign the rest of the papers."

At this point, I'm just going with it. Morris is still wearing the Santa hat Zoey made him, and the glittering sequins still dot his shoulders like snow. If this man is planning to throw me to the curb, he looks pretty damn blissed out about it.

We ride in silence after leaving Fingers's office. Morris is holding my hand tightly, a suspenseful silence filling the truck. We're almost back to the apartment when he makes a sudden turn and takes us down an unfamiliar street. He pulls into a driveway, and I recognize the house as the same one from the picture.

"This is mine?" I ask, still in shock.

It's dark outside now, but the exterior lights are on. The house is illuminated and looks welcoming, inviting. And it's big.

I reach for the door handle, assuming we're going inside, but Morris holds me fast.

"Wait," he says. He points to the glove box. "Can you grab the box in there?"

I look at Morris but pop the glove compartment.

"This one?" I pull out a small brown paper bag.

"Fuck no, not that one." Morris laughs and points to the glove box. "There's something else in there. The bag's for Leo. Christmas present I had made up. Didn't have the chance to wrap it yet."

"What is it?" I ask, curious and also delighted to know that Morris bought a gift for the kid who's become so important to us.

"Lower rocker," he says, as if I know what that means. "Go ahead, take a look."

I open the bag and pull out an embroidered patch that's shaped like a semi-circle. The word PROSPECT is stitched in thick letters.

"Prospect," I read. That much I know. "You're going to ask Leo to prospect with the club?"

Morris nods.

"Oh, Morris, he's going to flip out!"

Morris grins. "He sure will. Now go on back in there. There's something more for you. Wrapped box."

I reach into the glove box and find something else. It's a small box wrapped in sparkly red paper with a huge red bow tied around it.

"Go on," Morris urges, nodding at me.

I untie the bow and lift the top off the box to reveal a black satin box inside. "Oh. My. God," I sputter. "Morris…"

"Now, hear me out," he says, holding up a hand. "Alice, I want you. I want you more than I've ever wanted anyone or anything. But I know you need time. There's no rush. I've got a lot of shit going on with the club, expanding the businesses, building out the property. And I can't give up my space at the compound just yet. I'm a biker, through and through. But I want you and Zoey to have a home you can call your own. A place you get to kick me out of, lock the doors, and know you're safe. If you wanna dump my ass once you get settled, the house is yours. In your name and paid in full. You can cut out and sell it if you want, move to Denver, be with your sister."

I'm taking all of this in while I'm slowly opening the satin box. There's a beautiful emerald cut diamond ring inside.

"But if you decide you want me," he says, "I've got two more gifts for you." He nods toward the box and hands over the second envelope he took from Fingers.

"Morris…" My voice is shaking, and my stomach is doing flips. I can't decide what I want more—to pull that ring from the box and try it on, or open the envelope.

"Open the envelope," Morris urges.

That settles that. I set the ring securely in my lap and twist the fastener that holds the second envelope closed. As soon as I make out the words on the first page, I burst into tears.

"Oh fuck, Alice. No…" Morris looks concerned, worried. "I didn't mean… I don't have to. I just thought…"

I throw myself across the huge bench seat and wrap my arms around Morris's neck. "Yes," I cry, tears wetting Morris's beard as I kiss his face, his lips, his neck.

"Now, there's no rush, darlin'," he says, seeming to relax at my repeated cries of yes. "I just wanted you to know I'm here for the whole kit and caboodle. If you're mine, that means everything that comes with you is mine too. We don't have to rush, but there's no goddamn way I'd marry you and not officially adopt Princess Zoey."

The paperwork is unsigned, but it's ready. Once we sign all this, it will officially make us a family. Adoption papers making Morris legally, permanently, Zoey's dad.

He's giving me a ring that will officially make me Morris's old lady, which, after eight months of hanging around, I know means biker wife.

The house that's in my name will not just be the place I crash with my daughter. This house will be our home.

"You know what this means?" I say, looking over the paperwork.

"What's that?" Morris asks, holding me close.

"I know your first name now." I give him a nudge in the ribs, and we both laugh. "Dante. It's so…"

It's so not him. While being a good solid name, there's no way the man in front of me looks anything like a Dante.

He's totally a Morris.

"Stop. Come on," he says. "We've got people waiting on Chinese carryout."

And that's how it all ends.

My string of bad relationships.

My disappointment and self-doubt.

I have the promise of a happy ending and a real family for my daughter.

A man I can trust.

Friends and work and security.

Independence and, at the same time, love.

I let Morris slide the ring onto my finger, and he holds my hand to his lips, kissing me reverently.

For as many times as I've been knocked out of the nest, as many times as I've had my wings clipped, I believe I've now found my flock.

Lia, Leo, the girl crew.

Fingers and Midge.

Tiny and Morris.

My Zoey.

I think back to what Morris said so many months ago and how true it is for me now.

We ride, we crash.

We ride again, we crash again.

Sometimes we're lucky, and we don't fall far enough or hard enough to do any permanent damage. But most of the time, a fall means bad news. Real bad. You're fucked up so bad, you're not sure you're gonna make it. But if you wanna earn that patch and ride again, you get back up. You ride again.

And I, Alice Sparrow, have more than earned my broken wings.

Now it's time to fly.

Thank you for reading Broken Sparrow. I hope you love Morris and Alice as much as I do.

While they have a happily ever after, Leo and Lia's story is just getting started. They burn up the pages in **BROKEN DOVE**, another standalone novel in the Open Road series.

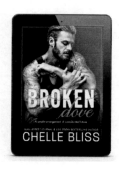

Lia Dove has always been a free spirit, living life to the fullest and never putting down roots. But after finding her birth father, along with a group of lovable, rowdy bikers, she can't imagine being anywhere else. Throw in a hot biker roommate who offers her no-strings-attached deal as the cherry on top and leaving becomes an afterthought.

Leo Hawk has never felt part of anything until he becomes a prospect in a local motorcycle club. But catching feelings for his roommate, who's also the club president's daughter, could spell disaster before he earns his patch.

But when the past comes back to haunt him thanks to his missing older brother, Leo will have to lean on his biker brothers for help, risking a future with the club and the woman he's grown to love.

Broken Dove is an interconnected standalone friends-to-lovers, motorcycle club romance, but can be read and enjoyed alone.

Tap here to read now **>> BROKEN DOVE**
or visit *menofinked.com/broken-dove*

LOVE SIGNED PAPERBACKS?

Visit *chelleblissromance.com* for signed paperbacks, ebooks, audiobook, and Bliss book merchandise.

Don't Miss Out!

Join my newsletter for exclusive content, special freebies, and so much more. Click here to get on the list or visit **menofinked.com/news**

Do you want to have your very own **SIGNED paperbacks** on your bookshelf? Now you can get them! Tap here to check out Chelle Bliss Romance or visit **chelleblissromance.com** and stock up on paperbacks, Inked gear, and other book worm merchandise!

Join over 10,000 readers on Facebook in Chelle Bliss Books private reader group and talk books and all things reading. Tap here to come be part of the family or visit **facebook.com/groups/blisshangout**

Want to be the first to know about upcoming sales and new releases? Follow me on Bookbub or visit bookbub.com/authors/chelle-bliss

OPEN ROAD SERIES

Book 1 - Broken Sparrow (Morris)
Book 2 - Broken Dove (Leo)
Book 3 - Broken Wings (Crow)
Book 4 - Broken Arrow (Arrow)

The Open Road series is interconnected with the
Men of Inked: Heatwave series. Learn more at
menofinked.com/heatwave-series

Also available in alternative paperback

WANT MORE MORRIS OR HOT READS?

If you haven't read the Men of Inked Heatwave, you're missing out. It's where Morris first appears along with the guys from the Disciples MC.

Download your **copy of FLAME** by visiting _menofinked.com/flame_

Want more ebooks? Turn the page!

ABOUT THE AUTHOR

I'm a full-time writer, time-waster extraordinaire, social media addict, coffee fiend, and ex-history teacher. *To learn more about my books, please visit menofinked.com.*

Want to stay up-to-date on the newest Men of Inked release and more? Join my newsletter.

Join over 10,000 readers on Facebook in Chelle Bliss Books private reader group and talk books and all things reading. Come be part of the family!

See the Gallo Family Tree

Where to Follow Me:

Made in United States
North Haven, CT
02 August 2024

55676284R00163